inside girl

ALL THAT GLITTERS

girl

inside girl

ALL THAT GLITTERS

a novel by **J. MINTER**

author of the insiders

BLOOMSBURY

BLOOMSBURY

Copyright © 2008 by J. Minter
and 17th Street Productions, an Alloy company

Published by Bloomsbury U.S.A. Children's Books
175 Fifth Avenue, New York, NY 10010
Distributed to the trade by Macmillan

Library of Congress Cataloging-in-Publication Data
Minter, J.
All that glitters : an inside girl novel / by J. Minter. — 1st U.S. ed.
p.   cm.
Summary: When winter break ends and Flan decides to return to her exclusive Manhattan
girls' school in spite of the spats she has had with another student, she is determined to
cement her popularity among her fellow students, no matter what it takes.
ISBN-13: 978-1-59990-257-9 • ISBN-10: 1-59990-257-5
[1. High schools—Fiction. 2. Schools—Fiction. 3. Popularity—Fiction. 4. Dating (Social cus-
toms)—Fiction. 5. New York (N.Y.)—Fiction.] I. Title.
PZ7.S3872Al 2008   [Fic]—dc22   2008007620

alloyentertainment
Produced by Alloy Entertainment
151 West 26th Street, New York, NY 10001

First U.S. Edition 2008
Printed in the U.S.A. by Quebecor World Fairfield
10 9 8 7 6 5 4 3 2 1

for J. Morphew and Destiny

epeat after me," SBB said. She was sitting half-in and half-out of a pair of Gucci riding pants with her eyes closed and her hand over her heart. "I, Sara-Beth Benny."

Camille and I gave each other a sly grin. We were standing in a mirrored private dressing room on the fifth floor of Bergdorf Goodman on 58th Street, surrounded by champagne flutes of Pellegrino and a tray of chocolate covered strawberries the shopgirl had brought in. It was the Sunday afternoon before classes started up at Thoney, and we were waiting for her to return with a wheeled rack of winter clothes we'd selected for some back-to-school shopping. In the meantime, SBB was making us vocalize our New Year's resolutions.

"Wait," Camille said, nudging me and giggling. "If it's *your* resolution, why do we repeat after you? We're not Sara-Beth Benny, last time I checked."

SBB opened one eye and looked at Camille. "Collective affirmation of resolutions has the highest rate of follow-through." She pinched Camille playfully on the arm. "Don't worry—we'll get to you guys next."

As someone who was used to indulging SBB's crazy ways, I gave Camille a nod and joined SBB on the gilded carpet. Camille plopped down next to me, and we followed the instructions.

"I, Sara-Beth Benny," we repeated, as mock-solemnly as we could.

In the three-way mirror in front of us, I could see our reflections from all angles. Camille was still glowing from her family's New Year's trip to Cabo, and SBB looked fresh faced from a week off from filming and a week on with her new boyfriend, actor-musician Jake Riverdale.

As I looked over at my reflection, I was pleased to see that I had my own sort of glow. It wasn't from a vacation tan, and it wasn't from a boy, but it was satisfying in a very Flan way. It had to do with my decision to start at Thoney this semester and, even though my excitement was tinged with a case of nerves, I was happy.

SBB continued. "I, Sara-Beth Benny, promise to donate a portion of all of my movie and TV royalties, as well as my perfume line profits, to help those in

Africa who are less fortunate than I. And maybe to adopt a child who needs love and whom I could cart around in one of those cute Karma Baby slings. And to grow at least six inches by July."

"Whoa," Camille said. "I was only going to try to start recycling more."

Just then, the shopgirl returned, wheeling in a giant clothing cart full of gorgeous-looking sweaters, pants, and slinky dresses. Instantly, we forgot our collective New Year's affirmation and pounced on the clothes like wild animals.

"Omigod," SBB said, grabbing a sheer polka-dotted dress from the middle of the rack. "Is this so 'Flan on the first day of school' or what?"

I held up the tiny Geren Ford dress to my body. It was asymmetrical, and it tied around the left shoulder with an almost nonexistent green silk strap. It was also no longer than my crotch.

"It's cute," I said, stalling as I searched for the right words so that I wouldn't offend SBB. "But it looks more like 'Flan gets thrown out of school before third period.'" My hand reached for a supercozy navy Autumn Cashmere drape sweater. "How about something more like this?" I said.

"Okay, Mister Rogers," Camille said, taking it from my hands and hanging it back up. "Believe me, I know that rocking the five-foot-ten frame does present its own set of fashion challenges, but I will not let you be a frump master on the first day of school." She rooted through the rack of clothes and pulled out a shrunken gray blazer with three-quarter sleeves and a really unique notched collar. "How about something like this?"

"*Cute!*" SBB and I said simultaneously.

"Ooh," SBB continued, looking at the label. "And it's my old costar Waverly James's new line. She was showing me how to wear it . . . there are these really cute leggings that go with this top. . . ." Her voice trailed off as her tiny body virtually disappeared into the rack of clothes.

"SBB," I said, sticking my head in after her. "Are you still in here?"

"Ta-da!" She jumped out, holding a pair of stretchy black leggings with a row of brass studs around the cuffs. She waggled them at me. "Terrick Zumberg, here you come!"

Camille squealed. "Um, speaking of New Year's resolutions! Flan, you *must* wear those leggings with this blazer on the first day of school. Because you know what happens on the first *night* of school, right?"

I shook my head. "Homework?" I asked hesitantly.

"No! All the Thoney girls go to David Burke's to

4

meet the Dalton boys for pizza—and then TZ will see you in *this*!"

I let my friends hold up the clothes against me and looked at myself in the mirror. The ensemble was totally my style, but I was suddenly feeling more than a little overwhelmed. It made me nervous that Camille just assumed I'd be up on all the Thoney protocol. And now there were all these expectations about impressing TZ, whom I'd barely seen since we'd hung out over Thanksgiving break in Nevis. All the old fears I thought I'd freed myself of came creeping back into my mind. What if I couldn't keep up with life at Thoney?

Camille must have sensed me getting tense. "Hey," she said, linking her arm through mine. "Don't stress. This semester is going to be amazing, whether or not you decide to grace TZ with your affection."

I looked in the mirror at my two best friends and nodded. "You're right. Thoney, the David Burke's pizza party—bring it on!"

"Of course Camille is right," SBB agreed. "Now try these on so I can envy your long legs even more."

I slipped into the leggings, and Camille handed me a long ribbed cotton tank with detailed stitching that fell well below my waist. When I pulled the blazer on over it and looked in the mirror, I felt instantly more self-assured. I tried to imagine a boy looking at me. I guess I did look pretty good.

"Hey, you guys," SBB called. She'd sneaked out of the dressing room and was standing at the edge of the shoe department, holding up a pair of Joie patent leather Mary Janes in one hand and a pair of caramel-colored Michael Kors boots in the other. "Flan, come here and try these on with that outfit."

Camille and I left the dressing room and stepped out into the bright, bustling floor of the shoe department. The Mary Janes looked pretty great with the leggings.

"Ooh," Camille said, holding one up to me and putting on a dramatic advertising voice. "This shoe will take you from study hall to evening ball."

"And right into the arms of *TZ*," SBB sang.

"*Shhh!*" I blushed and immediately looked around. It would be just my luck that TZ's cousin or grandmother would be shopping within earshot. Luckily, there were just the usual crew of personal assistants on their BlackBerrys and a bunch of overbearing Upper East Side mothers making their daughters try on "just one more pair" of Chloé loafers.

But then . . .

"I *thought* I recognized those voices," said someone behind me.

I spun around and immediately knew I hadn't been comprehensive enough in my coast-is-clear sweep of the store. Standing before me was my ex–best friend, Kennedy Pearson.

"I was just picking up my outfit for the first day of spring semester, and I couldn't help but overhear your little discussion in the dressing room."

I looked at Kennedy's clear plastic Bergdorf garment bag and was stunned to see the very same pair of black leggings that I had on. I could feel the blood rushing to my cheeks. If I ever had to put a single face on all my anxieties about returning to Thoney, that would be Kennedy's—and it would have the same smug look on it that Kennedy had right then.

She put her hand on my arm. "I just wanted to apologize, Flan."

"For what?" I said, moving my arm from her grasp. "For eavesdropping?" *For stealing my outfit? For being the devil incarnate?*

"No." She winced dramatically. "For having to be the one to tell you, when it's clear that you're really into TZ." She covered her face with her hand in faux-anguish. "How do I say this? I'm so sorry, Flan, but TZ and I are sort of together. As of New Year's."

There was a time when I wouldn't have known how

to respond to this. A time when my face would have turned red, and I would have had some whiny, embarrassing response like, "But I thought he liked *me*." But I had just spent that week in Nevis finally figuring out how to stand up to Kennedy, and I was determined not to revert back to sad-and-immobile-Flan again. I squared my shoulders, finally thankful for my height, and peered down at Kennedy's Laura Mercier made-up face.

"You know what, Kennedy? You can have him. Sounds like TZ is even flakier than you. You two deserve each other."

Kennedy's face flushed bright red and her glossy lips parted in shock.

"Wow, go Flan!" Camille whispered at my side. Then I waited, but it was like Kennedy couldn't find anything to say, and so we all just stood there, sniffing the perfume-scented air and waiting for her to back away.

And then, just as I was able to relax enough to start reveling in the fact that I had finally said the right thing at the right time, Kennedy's cell phone started to ring.

"Oh," she said, "that's TZ now." Putting the phone to her ear, she said, "Hold on a sec, honey." Then she turned back to me. "You know, Flan, some people might think you're 'brave' to come back to Thoney, but I personally think you're really, *really* going to regret it. Especially after that precious jealousy outburst you just had." Waving her leggings in my direction, she started toward the elevator. "Can't wait to see you Monday!"

"Oh, she's *going* to see you Monday," SBB shouted, hurling a wad of tissue paper from a nearby shoebox at Kennedy's receding back.

My legs started shaking in my studded leggings, and I grabbed Camille's and Sara-Beth's arms for support. I swallowed hard. This was *not* the fabulous start I'd envisioned for my New Year. What kind of mean little competition could I possibly have gotten myself into?

I'll be the first person to admit that my family is a little bit . . . unorthodox.

Growing up, most of my parent-teacher conferences took place via video conference call because my globetrotting parents couldn't be tied down long enough to swing by my elementary school for a chat about my first place win in the science fair.

Not that I'm complaining—after all, when I did get that blue ribbon for my analysis on why you should always talk to your plants while you water them, my parents flew me out to meet them for the weekend in Cape Town (or Buenos Aires, or Hong Kong, or wherever it was this time for a good old-fashioned Flood-style celebration).

Turns out, this legendary wanderlust is hereditary, because both my sister, February, and my brother, Patch, could literally be anywhere in the world at any given moment. We joke about how I'm the homebody, how I'm happiest curled up on our big suede couch in the living room, watching the flow of Manhattanites go by our Perry Street windows. But the truth is, I rarely am happier than when I'm home *with* the added bonus of my crazy family.

Sunday night happened to be one of those uncommonly lucky nights: the whole Flood crew was present . . . if only for a few fleeting hours.

"Yes, I'm calling to confirm a limo for five-thirty tomorrow morning," my brother was saying into his cell phone when I walked in the door with my shopping bags loped over my arm. "To Kennedy airport . . . Flight one hundred to Dubrovnik."

Even though it was five o'clock, Patch was wearing his gray silk Armani pajamas, and his dirty blond hair was sticking out in all directions from a recent nap. I met his raised palm with my own for a high five and started up the stairs.

In the bathroom I shared with Feb (on the rare occasions when she was actually around), I found my older sister rummaging through the cosmetically overstuffed cabinets. Her long, straight blond hair was piled up in a knot on top of her head and fastened with a giant green batik patterned scarf. She was speaking—very emphatically—into her phone.

"Of course, I have three hair straighteners, Jade," she said, counting the flatirons laid out on the tile floor. "I just can't find my adapter for Asia. So make sure you bring whatever we need for Cambodia. It's more humid there than Bungalow 8 on a Saturday night in July."

I was used to this flurry of activity from my siblings, and usually I'd plop down next to Feb and help her sort through her stash of adapters. But at the moment, I was feeling pretty wound up, too. My mind was still spinning with Kennedy's cutting words about her recent hook-up with TZ.

It was weird. I mean, TZ was a cool guy and everything, but mostly, he was someone for my friends to tease me about—not someone I genuinely wanted to date. So it wasn't jealousy I was feeling, the way that Kennedy had made it sound. It was just that I didn't want to give her any more ammunition that she could use to lord over me once school started.

I lay down on my canopy bed to recompose myself and, as if on cue, Noodles, the world's greatest Pomeranian puppy, made an appearance on my pillow, circled three times, and plopped down in my arms.

"Oh, Flan! I didn't hear you come in, dear." My mother's blond head appeared in my doorway, waving her nails out in front of her to dry. When she was in town on Sundays, her manicurist-waxist, Heleva, came downtown from Bliss to give my mom her special home treatments.

"How was shopping?" she asked, then held out a perfectly manicured hand. "Do you think *Keys to My Karma Red* was a bad choice? Be honest—is it too 'Garish Cousin Linda at the annual Flood regatta?'"

"Not at all; it's very classy," I told my mom. "More like 'Princess Grace hosts the Kennedys for dinner.'"

She nodded her head. "Good. I just got so caught up in *Bruno vs. Carrie Ann* that I barely paid attention to what Heleva was doing. I wouldn't want anyone at the Taj Mahal to look at your father and me and think 'tourist'—not that that would happen—but I'd hate to think it *could*." She looked at her watch. "Speaking of your father, he's going to be home in ten minutes . . . maybe. Definitely less than an hour. We're having a family dinner tonight."

"Really?" I asked, a little giddy. It was a rare thing for the five of us to be in the same area code, let alone the same room for a Sunday dinner.

"Of course, darling," my mom said. "We need to do a little celebrating in honor of your return to the female half of the family's alma mater."

* * *

An hour later, I was sitting at our dining room table watching the sun set over the West Village as my mom brought out heaps of food served on our best china.

"Did someone cook?" my father asked, looking suspiciously over the top of his Oliver Peoples horn-rimmed glasses at the gilt-edged china, which I'm not sure any of us actually recognized.

"Yeah, the sous chef at Otto," Feb said, retying her green scarf like a headband instead of a turban. "Mom had everything delivered."

My father nodded, as if this made much more sense than someone in our family actually preparing a meal. "Your mother is a genius," he said, brushing his salt and pepper hair off his forehead.

"That's where Flan gets it," Patch said as he walked into the dining room, tousled my hair, and took a seat next to me. He'd changed out of pajamas into a wrinkly T-shirt and a pair of hemp jeans; his hair still mussed in that just-fell-out-of-bed way. "You ready to knock their private school socks off tomorrow?"

I hesitated. If there was anyone in my family I'd tell about the horrific scene with Kennedy this afternoon, it would probably be Patch. He was the closest to my age, and he'd hung out with Kennedy a few times at parties his friends had thrown. But somehow the ugly topic of Kennedy Pearson didn't quite fit in with our very happy family dinner, so I just gave Patch my best private school grin and nodded.

"It'll be just like old times," I said. And despite my nerves about Kennedy's self-declared Thoney domination, I really was excited to return to private school. My first semester of public high school at Stuy had been really important for me, and not just because I got to go to a real high school football pep rally or because of the liberal dress code policy—which revealed the endless options of body piercing and confirmed for me forever that such adornment was so not my thing. It was because after a couple of not-so-great experiences, I learned that Camille and my old friends from Miss Mallard's were the girls with whom I wanted to make the rest of my high school memories.

Feb's BlackBerry beeped, bringing my mind back to the dinner table, and she sighed heavily as she chewed a big bite of escarole.

"Seriously?" She rolled her eyes. "In the future, someone please remind me to limit my travel with obsessive French designers. It's like Jade thinks we're packing for a year-long getaway to the moon. This is just a quick trip in and out of Cambodia." She fumbled with her scarf again and rewrapped it pashmina-style over her shoulders.

"Jade Moodswing?" my mom asked, cutting delicately into a slice of heirloom tomato pizza. "I just saw on TV that she was involved somehow with the president of Belgium."

"Purely speculation," Feb said. "Jade has already said *pas de comment* to *Le Figaro*." I bit back a laugh. Leave it to Feb to get involved in an international social scandal.

As we polished off the rest of the Otto feast, I got a slew of parting words of wisdom from each of my family members.

"Find your way to your classes first," Feb said after a bite of olive oil ice cream. "Then find out where your friends hang between classes. Every girl in that school knows how crucial it is to mark territory. And you know what they say: location, location, location."

"One word," Patch said, pointing his finger at me with a half-joking grin. "Upperclassmen."

"Study hard," my mom said, unabashedly tearing up now and using her napkin to wipe her eyes. "And show the school your beautiful smile."

My father looked at me last. "Just be yourself, Flan. Follow that advice and a Flood has nothing to worry about."

I leaned back in my chair and breathed a sigh of relief. I could always count on my family for good, calming advice when I needed it.

So why did Kennedy's mocking face keep popping into my head?

*B*right and early the next morning, I clung for my life to the overhead bar on the beyond crowded uptown 4 train. Usually I took a cab to school, but since I was all about fresh starts these days, I figured I'd start by breaking in my Metrocard.

Then again, maybe I should have known that expressing my independence via mass transit wasn't such a good idea, given how my morning had started out. So far, Noodles had turned the brand-new Bendel's cashmere socks Feb had given to me for Christmas into an argyle war zone on my bedroom floor. My flatiron had short-circuited the left side of our house, so I couldn't even make coffee or pop in my usual multigrain toast for a quick peanut butter and banana sandwich. Not that I felt like eating much anyway. My stomach felt like it might be tied permanently in a knot the size of Feb's green batik head scarf.

Now I was squished up against about a hundred other commuters, probably wrinkling version 2.0 of my back-to-school outfit (the studded leggings hanging in my closet just didn't look as appealing after I'd seen them in Kennedy's shopping bag).

Luckily Camille and SBB had been there to do conference call triage, and we'd come up with a pretty sweet alternative. I'd decided to go with the same notched blazer and white tank, but I paired them with gray leggings and a just-long-enough pleated schoolgirl skirt. The skirt had been my find of the season at Beacon's Closet, the funkiest consignment store in all of Williamsburg.

As the doors of the train thudded open, I clutched my Fendi messenger bag and made my way through the masses toward the exit at 86th Street.

I hurried across Park Avenue, clutching my coat against the cold wind, and instinctively glanced up at my ex-boyfriend Adam's apartment on East 88th Street. It'd been a couple weeks since our breakup, and we'd spoken only once or twice. Catching a glimpse of the football trophies lining his windowsill, I felt a tiny pang. Still, I had to admit, even as I waved shyly to his doorman, Adam—and my whole life back at Stuyvesant—felt pretty far away.

With four minutes to spare, I found myself jogging

up Thoney's majestic front steps. This place looked more like the Met than a high school. I'd been here once before, but I guess I'd never paid close attention to the building's haute aesthetics. Now there was just an ornate wrought iron gate between me and the five-story brick mansion where I'd be spending the bulk of the next three and a half years.

Hordes of chic girls I didn't know poured out of town cars and through the front doors. All of them looked chatty and exited, like there was an Intermix warehouse sale going on inside. My eyes searched for just one familiar face, but I couldn't make out a single girl I knew under the barrage of the latest outerwear from Searle.

Then, at my waist, I felt my iPhone buzz with a text from Camille. Thank God. Hopefully she'd just tell me where to meet her so I wouldn't have to enter the lion's den alone.

SNAFU AT DEAN & DELUCA. . . . CUTE BARISTA STRUCK DOWN BY FLU. NEW GUY TOTALLY LAGGING ON FROTHED MILK FOR MY MOCHA. SO SORRY—SAVE ME A SEAT AT ASSEMBLY!!!

So much for a familiar face. Hmm. Even under my peacoat, shearling hat, and Moschino all-weather boots, I found myself shivering. But wait. I could do this. This was what I'd wanted. All I had to do was take a deep breath and open the doors. The rest of my life was calling—and so was the tardy bell.

I pulled open the giant heavy door and stepped inside. Thoney was way nicer than stuffy, tapestry-laden Miss Mallard's, which I used to think was pretty ritzy. Dark purple drapes tumbled from the high ceilings down to the iridescent marble floors of the foyer. Large, framed composites showcased classes of Thoney alums over the years. A quick scan of the faces showed women from all walks of life—from four state senators to the current chair of Lincoln Center, all the way to the socialites of my generation, whose romps around town dotted Page Six of the *New York Post* on a daily basis. I couldn't help but feel a swell of pride when I saw my own mother's senior shot. Her black off-the-shoulder shell was so classic that not only was it still hanging in her closet, I'd worn it to the Bergdorf Christmas gala with SBB as well.

When I turned away from the photos, trying to mimic the confident smile my mom wore in her picture, I accidentally caught the eye of a girl wearing an iPod and a green headband in her curly mop of blond hair. She returned my grin.

"Love your blazer," she said, before disappearing into the horde of girls heading into the North Wing assembly room.

"Thanks," I said, fingering the buttons of my jacket. It didn't matter that she was already gone. I'd just had my first girly moment at Thoney. As I joined the stampede of girls funneling into the assembly, my boots clunked on the marble floor a little bit more happily than they had a minute before.

The auditorium was abuzz with post–winter break chatter. I could barely hear the bell ring over the chorus of all the "Omigod, I love your—" ringing out, and suddenly my "I'm confident" smile faltered. Even though Stuy had about a million more students than Thoney, the vibe there had always felt so much more diverse and mellow than this. There was something about so many of the same type of girls having the same type of conversation all in one room that was a tiny bit overwhelming. Almost dizzily, I sank into an open seat on a bench at the back of the room.

No sooner had I loosened my cranberry-colored Benetton scarf from around my neck than I felt a sharp pinch on my elbow. I spun around to see Camille's grimace as she practically yanked me off the bench.

"We don't sit here," she hissed. "Upperclassmen do."

For a second, I thought there might have been a tinge of real exasperation in her voice, but then she winked at me and tossed her long brown hair playfully as she pulled me onto a more permissible bench in the third row.

"I've never been so glad to see you in my life," I whispered to her. "Was I about to get thrown to the upper-class wolves?"

Camille nodded. "That's the senior bench. It's incredibly bad luck to sit there till you are one. You have no idea how insane the Thoney superstitions are."

"I guess not," I said, tucking my scarf into my bag.

"But you'll learn," Camille said happily and produced two Dean & Deluca coffee cups from her tote. "Hazelnut latte, no whip, right? Be stealthy"—she nodded toward a hovering teacher—"they don't call her Professor Daggers for nothing."

Before I could thank Camille for reading my caffeine-deprived mind, she nudged the girl to her left.

"Flan Flood," she said, gesturing toward me. "Meet your new crew. This is Harper Alden," she said, pointing to the wholesome, blond girl unbuttoning her black Searle coat to her left. "Watch out for this one. She's the captain of the debate team and she takes no prisoners."

"Omigod, don't scare her, Camille," Harper said, laughing and giving me a friendly wink. "Don't worry, Flan, I only bring out the claws at the podium."

Next to Harper was a gorgeous Filipino girl with amber-colored eyes and long black hair. "This is Amory Wilx, drama buff extraordinaire," Camille said as Amory curtsied dramatically in her seat.

Finally, Camille pointed to the same curly haired girl who'd complimented me in the foyer a few minutes ago. "And this is Morgan Burnette, resident DJ."

As Morgan turned off her iPod, I noticed that she was listening to the new Cat Power cover album that I'd been playing on repeat since I'd bought it the week before.

"We've heard so much about you from Camille," Harper said.

"All good things," Amory said, nodding enthusiastically. "We've basically been dying to meet you."

"Still *loving* your blazer," Morgan said, bobbing her head to some unheard beat, as if she hadn't just turned off her headphones.

These girls were so immediately likable that I quickly felt at ease. And when I glanced across the aisle, I was happy to see that I recognized my friend Olivia from Miss Mallards sitting next to two of her friends, Dara and Veronica, whom I'd met when Olivia and I bumped into each other while shopping this past fall. I waved at them and all three waved back with big smiles and fingerless gloves.

When the doors at the front of the auditorium opened and a group of stern women in navy blazers walked in, a hush fell over the crowd. I had never seen so much gossip evaporate so quickly. Camille had mentioned that the faculty at Thoney could be severe, but this bunch looked like it was their mission to leave a sea of anxious, quaking girls in their wake.

A silver-haired woman with a loosely swept French twist and porcelain skin took the podium.

"Welcome back, girls," she said with perfectly polished Manhattan enunciation. "I trust you all had relaxing and enjoyable winter holidays."

"Yes, Headmistress Winters," the room sang back collectively.

"Many of you are returning students, but for those of you who are new, it may do you well to hear some ground rules—rules that are taken quite seriously here at Thoney. Starting with the dress code . . ."

Winters didn't mince words. I was pretty sure that the dress code at Thoney was going to be a whole lot stricter than at Stuy, where basically anything went except bandannas and gang colors. But just as she was getting to the details of Thoney's sartorial protocol (which basically amounted to nothing overly provocative and she'd "be the judge of that"), Camille lightly touched my arm.

"*Our* dress code is what matters," she said in a low whisper. "A group of us started Theme Day Thursdays. An e-mail blast goes out Wednesday night with the details. It's so fun—you'll totally love it. During finals last semester we did Bad Christmas Sweater Day. It was hilarious. Oh, and Fridays we always wear jeans."

I nodded, wondering half-jokingly if I should be taking notes. Because it seemed like for every official rule the headmistress had to offer to the group, Camille overruled it with a social rule of her own.

"Cafeteria commandments," Camille went on, as the headmistress gave her honor code spiel. "Never get anything but the salad bar. Or the mac and cheese. Or the fries. Basically, all lunchroom meat and dairy products are frowned upon."

"And we always sit at the third table in any room we go into," Harper leaned over to whisper, her curtain of blond hair hiding her moving lips from Winters. "It's easier to remember that way. Third bench in the auditorium, third table by the windows in the cafeteria, third study cluster in the library. You'll start to see that all the groups sit in similar places, so you'll always know where to find the various cliques—and there are a *lot*."

I squinted at them. "Is it really that divided?"

Camille shrugged. "You'll see. It's not that bad. For the most part, everyone gets along. It just, you know, makes it easier to keep organized."

Just then Headmistress Winters bellowed out, "*Organization* is the key to your success at Thoney," and Camille, Harper, and I had to bite our lips to keep from laughing.

"Okay," Camille went on, sneaking out her BlackBerry. "I made you a list of the clubs that are cool to join and those that are kinda off-limits. I'll e-mail it to you before the Activities Fair this afternoon. Now, I'll just have to give you the bare-bones basics about who's social suicide to talk to."

I think Camille may have noticed my wide eyes— social suicide? Just from talking to someone? She put her hand on my knee.

"I know, I know, it sounds completely ridiculous even to say it out loud, but I'll just throw it all out there so you won't say I didn't warn you. This is Thoney, after all."

I nodded. It certainly was. Had I been stupid to think that I'd be busy enough keeping track of my new locker combination and what room my French class was in? Obviously there would be a social protocol to follow here, just like there had been at Miss Mallards, and even at Stuy.

I took a covert swig of my latte and squeezed Camille's hand for her to go on.

"Okay," she whispered, "the obvious first person to steer clear of . . ."

Just then, from across the room, I felt a pair of icy green eyes settle on mine. *Kennedy.* I knew I was bound to see her today, but whatever Camille was saying washed right over my head as Kennedy flipped her wavy black hair from side to side. How could she make such an innocent gesture look so deadly? How long had she been staring at me? And who was that bombshell sitting next to her with the similarly bitchy look on her face?

"Hold up," I asked Camille. "Who's the satanic model over there?"

Camille followed my eyes. "Oh, Kennedy's friend? That's Willa Rubenstein. One word: rhinoplasty. Four additional words: Don't mess with her. Her father owns the Rubenstein Fund, and she's not afraid to play the daddy trump card in a pinch."

Just then Willa's blond hair spun around, and she looked down her perfect nose at us. She pressed a finger dramatically to her lips and narrowed her blue eyes with an exaggerated shushing sound.

Suddenly I felt the whole room turn to stare at me. There was a rustling and a murmuring and even the headmistress looked up from her rule book.

"I trust there's no problem, girls, so early in the semester. Am I correct?"

I bit my pinky nail. It sounded less like a question and more like an icy command.

"No problem, Headmistress Winters," answered a sing-songy chorus of voices. Well, at least there seemed to be one front that the Thoney girls were united on.

Camille shrugged and rolled her eyes at me conspiratorially. I wanted to roll mine back, but I felt Kennedy still staring me down. I tried to avoid looking back, but her glare was like a magnet. Just before the bell rang to dismiss the assembly, we locked eyes once more and Kennedy's arched eyebrows and snarky wink could only mean one thing.

What happened in Nevis wasn't going to stay in Nevis. I was on her territory now . . . and this was war.

Chapter 4

"Okay, take these stairs to the third floor and hang a left," Camille was saying minutes later in the hallway as she sketched a rough map on the back of her Dean & Deluca napkin. "Avoid the temptation to write on the Welcome Back Wall"—she drew an X over its location in the east wing—"it's controlled by the Student Senate, and who cares about them? And *never* use the bathroom at the end of the hall."

"Couldn't agree more," Amory said with a shudder. "Jenna Davidson used to Nair her mustache in there last year, and let's just say the scent has lingered."

I laughed, remembering how poor Jenna had had that mustache problem since the fourth grade at Miss Mallards. It was cool how quickly I was bonding with Camille's friends—but it also made me a little nervous to realize that as soon as Camille was done with her napkin mapmaking, she and Amory would scoot off to gym together, and I'd be left to roam the halls on the way to first period English all by myself.

Camille put the finishing touches on the map, sticking her tongue out as she drew, just like she'd done ever since we were swapping Bratz coloring books back in the day.

"*Voilà!*" she said, handing over her masterpiece, which had dotted lines to take me through my classes and which showed me where to meet her and the other girls in the gym after school for the Activities Fair.

"Thanks again," I said, giving both girls air-kisses. "Wish me luck!"

"Naturals like you don't need luck," Camille said as the two of them disappeared around the corner.

I followed the route to my first class, breathing through my mouth as I walked past the bathroom, and stepped inside a brightly lit room looking out over Madison Avenue. The first thing I noticed was that, unlike every classroom back at Stuy, these walls were not plastered with posters of cheesy motivational quotes set against snowy mountaintops. Here the walls were tastefully decorated with framed quotations from famous works of literature—some of which I recognized, many more of which I didn't.

There was no "third table" to sit at, just a cluster of desks, and I wanted to sit somewhere not too close to the front. I spotted an open seat in the middle of the room and moved toward it. I had just plopped down when I noticed Mattie Hendricks taking out her notebook to my left.

The last time I'd seen Mattie was in Nevis, and I remembered being happy to watch her let loose at a couple of the parties. I'd always liked Mattie, even though some of the girls called her "The Barker" behind her back. So what if she had a slightly awkward and badly timed laugh? She was sweet. Today she was wearing her standard issue Mattie uniform: a white Gap T-shirt and the same straight leg jeans she'd had since middle school.

"Hey, Mattie," I said, hanging the strap of my bag over the back of my seat.

"Flan!" she called with her usual enthusiasm. "I heard you were coming back to private school, but now that you're here, I can't believe it. This place needs you!" Her barking laugh rang out across the room.

I chuckled with Mattie to be nice, even though nothing funny had happened. I was also looking around the room to get a feel for the other girls in the class. They didn't look too scary. Actually, they looked pretty normal, just trying to squeeze in one last text message or nail file session before the bell rang. I'd been hoping Olivia might be in my class. We'd had English together back at Miss Mallards, and our notebooks had been filled with more games of Would You Rather than notes on Edgar Allan Poe.

"So, what's the scoop on freshman English here?" I asked Mattie.

"Oh, it's a breeze," she said, waving her hand at me. "You'll totally be fine. You like Shakespeare, right?"

"Uh, sure. 'To be or not to be,'" I stammered, trying to remember what little I knew of Shakespeare from Miss Mallards, although I didn't actually know where I'd pulled the reference from.

"Oh, we've already done *Hamlet*. I think we're picking up with *The Merchant of Venice*, even though *Romeo and Juliet* is totally my favorite. I'm such a romantic," she said, breaking out the bark-laugh for the second time. "Speaking of romance, are you going to go to the pizza party tonight with the Dalton boys?"

"Oh," I said, trying to figure out how to field this one. I hadn't had time to hear Camille's list of social suicide no-no's, but if I had, I would guess that The Barker would be near the top. But as I looked at

Mattie's big grin and eagerly clasped hands, I found myself nodding. Social demarcations be damned, right? I hadn't come back to Thoney to be snotty, and I could use all the friends I could get. "Sure," I found myself telling Mattie, "I'll be there. You should head over for some pizza, too."

"Oh, I really wish I could, but I have to dog-sit for my neighbor's cockapoo tonight," Mattie said, laughing so loudly that I could feel the rest of my new classmates staring at us both.

And of course, at that moment, Kennedy paraded in with Willa in a cloud of Betsey Johnson perfume. Both of them set down their corresponding Marc Jacobs leather satchels, then turned toward Mattie and me with correspondingly raised eyebrows. Somehow the room seemed quieter now that they were there, and each of my classmates was giving Kennedy and Willa the type of once-over glance that I usually reserved for models at Fashion Week.

If Kennedy noticed the attention, she didn't show it. Instead, she merely cocked her head at me and said, "So great that you two BFFs picked up right where you left off. Care to share what's so hilarious?" Her voice was sickeningly fake. "Or is it an inside joke that only you two could possibly find funny?"

But before I even had a chance to flub my second

Kennedy interaction of the day, in walked a pencil-thin man in a tweed coat and boxy glasses who I guessed was Mr. Zimmer.

"Welcome back, everyone," he said, taking a sip of coffee before leaning against his desk. "And welcome especially to our new student"—he looked down at his notes—"Flan Flood." When he looked up he scanned the room, saw my unfamiliar face, and gave me a warm smile. "Joining us from Stuyvesant, isn't it?"

"Yes," I said, blushing for no reason and feeling the whole room's eyes on me.

"And what were you studying at Stuyvesant?" he asked.

My brain went totally dead as I tried to remember a single thing I'd done to get that A on my English final last semester.

"Um," I said, fiddling with the buttons on my blazer. "We just read *Animal Farm*?" I felt my voice rise up in a question, and I wanted to say something else to not sound like such a nervous mute. "I really liked the way George Orwell satirizes communism."

Mr. Zimmer nodded. "I do, too. You'll find, however, that the curriculum at Thoney is not quite as progressive as your old school's. We're still stuck in the sixteenth century with Shakespeare. We shall begin this semester with *The Merchant of Venice*.

Everyone open the paperback you picked up as you came into class."

I looked around at the other twenty girls in the class, who all seemed to have the book in their hands. Very quietly, I got up and went to the front door to get the book while everyone watched.

English had always been one of my favorite subjects, and even if the Thoney curriculum was going to be a total switching of gears from what we'd been reading at Stuy, I figured I could handle it. After all, Mattie had said the class was a breeze, right? So why was I getting so flustered?

"Who would like to read the beginning of Act One?" Mr. Zimmer asked.

As one of the nail filing girls cleared her throat and began to read, I had to feel impressed by how assured she sounded plowing through the Shakespearean verse. But by the time I finally found where we were on the page, she was already reading the last line.

"Thank you, Maya. Very nice," Mr. Zimmer said. "Last semester, we discussed the purpose of an opening act, how to see it as an introduction that sets the proverbial stage for what's to come in the rest of the play. With that in mind, how can we make sense of this particular passage?"

Whoa. Mr. Zimmer might as well have been talking

in Shakespearean English. I was slinking down in my seat and praying that he wouldn't call on me when I realized, to my surprise and slight horror, that he wouldn't *have* to call on me. Half the class had their hands raised to answer.

Was I the only one who was lost?

As Mattie and even Kennedy were called on to answer Mr. Zimmer's questions, I realized: Yes, apparently I *was* the only one who didn't know exactly what was going on. I mean, I knew the gist of *The Merchant of Venice*, but that was mostly because I'd seen SBB's modern retelling, *Loan Shark of Venice Beach*. But all I'd heard for months was how hot her kissing scene with Penn DiMontagne had been, and since none of that was happening in Act One of the actual play, I had very little to add to the discussion going on in class.

Mr. Zimmer continued, "Now, who can tell me about the agreement that Antonio and Bassanio come to by the end of Act One? Flan, would you like to weigh in?"

I gulped. It sounded like an easy question. But with the whole class's focus suddenly shifted toward me, all I could think about was SBB lamenting how she and Penn never could quite recapture their passion off-screen.

I tried to block the image of the two of them making out in that one scene on the boardwalk so I could look at Mr. Zimmer and respond like a capable, intelligent girl. But I just kept seeing the way Penn brushed his blond hair out of his eyes before he leaned in to kiss SBB. After thirty painful seconds of dawdling, the only answer I could come up with was a very timid "Um . . ."

"Hmm," Mr. Zimmer said. "Someone else, then?"

Without missing a beat, Willa jumped in. "'Try what my credit can in Venice do,'" she recited from memory. "He wants to use Antonio's street cred for collateral. It's right here on the page," she said, shrugging carelessly in her baby blue cashmere shrug.

"Mmm. Yes, excellent, Willa," Mr. Zimmer said.

Street cred? Excellent? I wondered whether everyone in this school was drinking the "Bow down to Kennedy and Willa" Kool-Aid. Still, watching Willa blow off the question as utterly obvious, I felt like the class über-dunce. Why had I totally choked?

I dropped my eyes into my book and wished I were anywhere but here. I ran my eyes over the words another time, but the language was still swimming around in my head. All I wanted was to catch one phrase that made any sort of sense.

Just then, Mattie slyly dropped a folded sheet of paper on my desk.

TO FLAN, it said on the outside.

What was this? A pity note from The Barker? That would be a great way to start out the semester. Surely, Camille would have a rule against accepting this. But when I opened up the paper, I saw that the note wasn't from Mattie at all—what was written on the inside was far worse than anything Mattie could have thought of. But here, finally, were words I actually understood.

YOUR PERSONAL ACT ONE IS LOOKING A LITTLE TRAGIC. PERHAPS IT'S TIME TO GET THEE TO A TUTOR. —XOXO, KENNEDY

ACT I, SCENE II (MODERN ENGLISH VERSION)
Unsuspecting Manhattanite returns to
private school in attempt to make life
easier for herself. Finds struggle and
uncertainty waiting on the front steps.
Seeks trouble unintentionally. Seeks
tutor. Seeks happy ending to epic first
day.

                    SETTING
Student Activities Fair, Thoney
Gymnasium, Upper East Side Manhattan

*Enter Peppy Student Senate kid with high
ponytail and argyle shift dress.*

            PEPPY STUDENT SENATE KID
Hi! Welcome to the spring semester Student

Activities Fair! Here's your packet! And your Thoney ballpoint pen! And your window sticker—cute, huh? Please proceed in a counterclockwise motion around the gymnasium, and feel free to sign up for as many activities as you like!

HEROINE
Oh. Um. Thanks. Thank you.
Counterclockwise, did you say? Okay.

Somehow I had made it through the first day of school, rebounding slightly after the embarrassment of this morning's Shakespearean stumping. But what I saw when I entered the Thoney gymnasium at three forty-five on Monday afternoon was a whole different kind of overwhelming.

The place was insane. Sure, it showed some signs of being a high school gym—there were basketball hoops, free throw lines painted on the floor, retractable bleachers, and bad fluorescent lighting high up in the rafters. But if there's one thing the Upper East Side knows how to do, it's upgrade.

The overhead lights had been shut off, and the room was lit by a hundred soft-white antique street lamps. Individual wooden booths had been wheeled in and set up in concentric circles around the room. Each was decorated by a painted clapboard sign designating which club, team, or organization it represented. Clusters of girls with megawatt smiles and VOSS bottles in their hands beckoned those milling about to approach their booths and sign up. Bite-sized burgers and veggie sushi rolls went around on silver trays. And a deep gold carpet had been rolled around the booths so that it felt like you were following a yellow brick road toward your extracurricular dream destination.

I guess the sight of it all was sort of thrilling. I could totally dig the man in the beret flipping crepes at the French Club booth. And the Fashion Club's mini-runway was attracting more open-mouth stares than the Saks windows at Christmastime. But as I started walking—counterclockwise—around the room, the conversations I overheard brought me back to reality. Sure, the execution of this fair was award-worthy, but underneath the soft lighting, I was starting to see that this whole event was yet another Type-A UES spectacle.

"It just won't work," I heard a brunette in a red poncho and tortoiseshell Salt Works glasses say as she fiddled with her Trio. "I already have Key Club on Monday afternoons, riding on Tuesdays and Thursdays, and drama practice on Wednesdays. My masseuse asked me not to commit myself on Fridays so I can have *some* detox time. You're going to have to switch the Latin Club to a power lunch or I don't see how I'll be able to fit it in."

At the next booth, a Korean girl in a tailored suit and funky jewelry was facing her almost identically clad friend with crossed arms.

"No, I already told you. I was secretary last year. If I don't get at least treasurer this year, I'll never be president by senior year."

I kept walking, past a slew of other frantic voices looking for the Pilates club, the technology club, the Susan G. Komen breast cancer philanthropy club. Everyone in the room seemed to be in a hurry to pump up their college résumés. Coming to a high school like Thoney was a boost to any application, but it seemed like the student body here was still pretty cutthroat about securing a place at Harvard or Yale after graduation.

But all I wanted right now was to find my friends, sign up for a low-maintenance club or two, and debrief on how intense this place was while simultaneously gearing up for the Dalton pizza party later this afternoon. Where was Camille? The dotted line on the map she'd drawn me this morning only extended as far as the entrance to the gym. With the number of girls-on-a-mission in this room, I was beginning to worry that I might never find her.

I started to push my way through Roberto Cavalli tote bags and Halogen down jackets with as much vigor as the other girls when suddenly, I hit a roadblock. A very tall, very muscular, and somewhat scary-looking roadblock.

"Whoops," I said, taking a step away from the girl I'd just run into. "I'm sorry, I was just—"

"You're new," said the girl. She was sporting a gray zip-up hoodie with Thoney spelled out across the chest. Her long dirty blond hair was pulled back and, despite her intimidating frame, she had great cheekbones and friendly hazel eyes.

"Um, yeah," I stuttered. I still wasn't used to the fact that almost everyone else in this school knew each other—and that I stuck out because I didn't. "I'm Flan Flood," I said. "I just transferred from Stuyvesant."

"Cool," she said, nodding and flipping her ponytail over her shoulders. "Stuy has a killer field hockey team. Did you play?"

I shook my head. "No," I said, thinking that the field hockey girls at Stuy were all super intense and sporty and looked, well, a lot like this girl. Not that it was a bad thing. Suddenly feeling judgmental and guilty, I said, "But I used to see them practicing a lot. They looked pretty good."

The girl stuck out her hand. "I'm Ramsey Saybrook, captain of our freshman team. Have you ever thought about playing? We're not as hard-core as the Stuy team, but we could really use some height," she said, pointing at my frame as she talked.

I'd never thought about joining a sports team before, but I had spent many summers in the Hamptons playing roller hockey with Patch and his friends—once I gave Arno an accidental black eye when things got heated during a game-winning goal.

And hey, why not give field hockey a try? New year, new school, new activities, right? Ramsey seemed cool enough, and she did mention the team being more low-key than the one at Stuy, which was definitely a good sign.

I shrugged and nodded my head. "Sure," I said. "I'd love to sign up."

"Killer," Ramsey said, sounding genuinely enthused. "Let me get your e-mail, and I'll let you know about practice and everything."

After saying goodbye to Ramsey, I felt like I'd accomplished my extracurricular goals for the day. Now I just wanted to find Camille and the girls and maybe snag a crepe.

"Flan! Yoo-hoo—over here," I spun around in the direction of the voice and grinned when I saw Morgan waving me over. Camille and Co. were clustered—amazingly—right in front of the crepe stand. I *so* loved these girls.

"Hey, guys," I said, wading through the booths to get to them.

"How was your first day?" Camille asked. "Oh my God, have a bite of this banana Nutella thing—it's to die for."

I nibbled a bite from her crepe and said, "I guess you could say I'm still getting adjusted."

"Oh, but it's only your first day," Amory said, tugging on the brim of her black newsboy hat.

"And we're all still in winter break mode, so everyone's a little out of it." Morgan nodded as she fast-forwarded through a song on her iPod.

"Don't worry, you'll settle in fast. And we're here to help," Harper agreed.

Camille looped her arm through mine. "Did you guys sign up for any clubs yet? I just can't decide between yoga and Pilates. I mean, really, what's the difference?"

"I put in my time at the debate booth and managed to argue a few new people into joining the team," Harper said, tugging on her heather gray vest and looking pleased.

"Good work, Har," Amory said, shifting her Prada knapsack to the other shoulder. "I found out that auditions for the spring play are next week. We're doing *Cat on a Hot Tin Roof*." She beamed. "And I'm dying to play Maggie."

"I talked to Ms. Bridge about the radio station," Morgan added. "They're going to let me DJ on the station's Web site Thursday nights."

"I signed up for field hockey," I said, glad to be able to contribute to the conversation with my very involved friends. "I've never played before, but I think it'll be fun—"

"You did not!" Camille said, wide-eyed. "Didn't you get my e-mail?"

I shook my head. The day had been so crazy, I hadn't even had a chance to look at my iPhone.

"What's the big deal?" I asked. "I met this girl Ramsey, and she seemed really nice. . . . Kinda scary, but enthusiastic, and she said they needed more tall girls."

"Flan, Flan, Flan," Camille said as a teeny brunette munching on a raspberry crepe skirted around us.

"Jeez," I said, watching all the other girls shake their heads. "Did I already break another cardinal Thoney rule?"

"It's just that, um, Kennedy *and* Willa are on the team," Camille said. "And they are *fierce*."

Morgan nodded. "I heard Willa's father made her sign up so she could take out her 'aggression' in a productive way."

Suddenly there was a field hockey ball–sized lump lodged in my throat.

"Well, I can't back out now," I said, looking at Morgan's, Amory's, and Camille's worried eyes. "I've already signed up, and Ramsey said the first practice is tomorrow."

"Do you really want to play?" Camille asked. She bit her lip and cocked her head to the side, studying my face.

"Sort of," I said. "I mean, I did. And I don't want to let Kennedy or Willa stop me just because they're being so vicious, but . . ."

Camille looked at me in her Camille way.

My lips curved into a smile. "Are you having one of your ideas?"

"You could call it that," she said, smiling. "Would it make you feel any better to have a field hockey sidekick? I think I've still got my old stick from summer camp in our storage unit somewhere."

I couldn't bob my head "yes" fast enough.

"Have I mentioned before that you're a lifesaver?" I said.

"Well, girls," Camille said, wrapping her red scarf

around her neck. "That's settled. I think we've suffi-ciently conquered the Activities Fair. Who's ready for some pizza?"

"And boys!" Amory added.

"Me!" The rest of us chimed in at the same time, although I had to admit that I hoped one of the boys wasn't going to be TZ. . . .

A word to the wise: If you think you can cruise right through the accessories section at Bloomingdale's with four Thoney girls at your side and still make it to a pizza party on time, you're kidding yourself—it's just not going to happen.

"Oh my *God*," Amory squealed as we attempted to hurry across the white marble floors toward the David Burke's on the other side of the store. "Was I not just saying I needed a rabbit trim hat to go with the muff my sister gave me for Christmas? What are the odds? I have to see if they have it in black."

With reflexes like a cat, Camille snatched Amory by the scruff of her Tory Burch turtleneck to prevent her from diving face-first into the shockingly large rabbit trim section of the store.

"Nuh-uh, A. You promised you would show some self-restraint," Camille said, laughing. "We're already late."

"We can be five minutes later," Amory said, still pawing at the hat.

"We told the boys we'd be there twenty minutes ago," Camille said.

"Camille's right," Harper agreed, checking her metallic red BlackBerry to see what time it was. "We don't want Kennedy and Willa stealing our seats."

"What?" Morgan asked loudly, lifting one of her ear buds out of her ear to tune in to our conversation. "What about feeling out beats?" I could hear one of the new Nada Surf songs blasting out of the loose bud.

Harper shook her head and laughed at Morgan, as if this type of misunderstanding happened all the time. She pressed the pause button on Morgan's iPod and spoke into her non-headphoned ear. "Let's get a move on."

But at that moment, in a glass case across the aisle, Camille spotted a Ralph Lauren watch that I knew she'd been scoping out online for a couple of weeks. Instantly, she released Amory and grabbed my hand so we could both look at the watch.

"This is exactly the one I wanted," Camille said, clutching the glass case. "The Web site said it was out of stock, but now I can just get it here!"

This was what I loved about these girls. In my old circle of friends at Stuy, it always seemed like we were playing the same roles. In any given situation, Judith would act the part of the mostly loveable grump, Meredith would be the distractible and up-for-anything free spirit, and I would find myself somewhere in the middle, straddling the two extremes to make sure everyone stayed happy. But it seemed like no matter what happened, these girls pretty much went with the flow—with smiles on their faces to boot.

"But *Camille*," I teased, smiling myself. "Now we're twenty-*one* minutes late to the pizza party."

"Enough with the shopping!" Harper said. "Raise your hand if you're starving." She extended her own long, tan arm in the air, her charm bracelet sliding down to her elbow.

Morgan grinned and waved her iPod. "Yes!"

I grabbed the hands of the shopping bug–stricken Camille and Amory and pulled them out of the accessories section without any further delays.

As we stepped into David Burke's, we were greeted by the whimsical décor that always made me wonder whether I was in a restaurant or at the Big Apple Circus. The deep red booths were full of chatting Manhattanites who were just as consumed by what was in their Big Brown Bags as they were by the cheesecake lollipops on their plates. Waiters with trays of colorful, vertically stacked food whizzed along the black and white gingham print floor as we made our way to the back.

The boys had claimed an area by the window facing Third Avenue. When we first spotted them clustered around a table with extra chairs pulled up for us, I was surprised to feel my heart pick up and my cheeks flush.

My eyes were immediately drawn to TZ, who was waving his arms in the air, telling some story that was making all the other guys crack up. He was wearing a Burberry scarf and a green blazer that matched his eyes, and when he saw us getting closer, he grinned and nodded his head—guy-speak for hello.

To his left was Alex Altfest, who I still got weirdly nervous in front of ever since I'd overheard him tell my friend Olivia that he thought I was cute over Thanksgiving.

"We were wondering when the reason for the party would show up," Alex said now, holding his hand up for me to high-five. His black hair was cut short and his vintage Kinks T-shirt looked pretty cool—even though I was sure ripped clothes were against the Dalton dress code.

"Some of us got a little distracted by the fact that we had to walk through Bloomies to get here," I said as I slapped Alex's hand.

Alex nodded and flicked one side of his mouth up in a smile. "I've got a sister with the very same problem."

Just then, I felt two hands on my shoulders and looked up to see buffer-than-buff Danny Kaeffer attempting to nudge me over to the next seat.

"Hey, Flan," he said. "Think we can squeeze in a few more chairs?"

"Sure," I said, looking up to see who else had walked in. I waved when I saw shy Rob Zumberg, TZ's cousin who'd serenaded us with his guitar-playing most nights when we were in Nevis. I was doubly psyched to see Xander Ross at his side, still wearing his Dalton tie. Xander had been Camille's first true crush, and let's just say she was still waiting for her chance to cash in. Now she was twirling her hair around her finger and looking up at him with her big hazel eyes. He smiled widely at her, and I felt pretty confident that her chances were looking good.

As I helped Danny and Alex pull up a couple more chairs, I was thinking what a fun crowd this was. My nerves had settled, and I was ready to plop down between Alex and TZ and feast on the best arugula and prosciutto pizza this side of the park . . . when all of a sudden, TZ boomed, "Hey! You two finally made it. Danny, pull up two more chairs."

Before I even looked up, I knew from the tone of his voice and the stiffening of Camille beside me that the new arrivals to our peaceful little soiree would be none other than my future field hockey stick–wielding partners, Kennedy and Willa.

Whatever sway the two of them had over the girls in my English class this morning, let's just say it was doubly apparent with the guys tonight. Within seconds, Kennedy had sidled over and wedged herself directly between me and TZ.

"Oh Flan, please," she said in my ear, grabbing the back of the chair where I was about to take a seat. "You don't have to keep my seat warm. It's sweet, but entirely unnecessary . . . kind of like you."

"Get over yourself, Kennedy," I whispered back.

Alex pointed at the chair where Kennedy had sat down and said, "You trying to get away from me already?"

I blushed, but before I could answer, three waiters with trays full of pizza arrived. Everyone had to musical-chair their way around the table, which was made for about seven fewer people. Danny shoved down and there was one remaining chair right next to Alex, but just as I was about to sit down, Willa beat me to it.

"Aw, Flan, thanks for knowing just when to get out

of the way." She gave me an icy wink and plopped down with her knees against the table to show off her yellow python skin Gucci boots.

So that was how I ended up sitting on Camille's lap at the other end of the table until both of our legs fell asleep.

"Remember how Patch used to give us dead legs all the time when we were little?" Camille laughed as she shook red pepper flakes onto her pizza.

I shuddered. "Totally. And this feeling is just a tad too reminiscent," I said. "I'll go grab another chair."

When I stood up, Alex signaled me over to his side of the table. As I walked around Danny, Rob, and Willa to reach him, I tried to think of something witty to say. But just then, my foot caught on something.

I felt the fall happening in slow motion: my hand reaching out to try to grab the table, the slimy cheese of the pizza I'd grasped instead, Camille's long, low "*Noooo*" as I went down. Out of the corner of my eye, I saw the glint of one very yellow python boot tipped out at a dangerous angle.

Then I was on the ground, with half a black truffle pizza in my lap and no chance at all of brushing this one off lightly.

Within seconds, Camille, Morgan, Rob, and Alex were at my side, helping me up and dabbing pizza sauce off my blazer. Suddenly, Kennedy was there, too, doing a poor imitation of dusting crumbs off my skirt.

"So embarrassing, Flan," Willa called out loudly from her seat at the table while Danny chuckled. "Are you okay?"

Before I could answer, another less-saccharine voice hissed in my ear.

"Down in the dumps so soon? I told you you'd regret coming back," Kennedy said with a perfectly glossed smirk.

Before I could snap back, a huffy waiter broke us up with his dustpan and broom.

"Step away from the pizza—stat," he ordered.

"Wow, Flan, are you sure you're okay?" Camille asked as we all stepped away from the carnage. Everyone else sat down at the table and tore into the pizzas that I hadn't taken down with me.

"Yeah, but I think this day needs to end *now*. Tell everyone 'bye for me." I gave a sympathetic Camille a couple bills to cover the ruined food and carefully stepped out of the klutz spotlight with a parting wave to Morgan, Amory, and Harper.

As soon as I reached the restroom, I pulled out my iPhone and texted the one person who I knew could come to my rescue.

SERIES OF SOCIAL SNAFUS. SOS.

*T*en minutes later, a black Escalade slowed to a stop in front of the main entrance of Bloomingdale's. The back window scrolled down and SBB popped most of her tiny upper body out of it.

"Hello, my love," SBB chirped. She waved her hands wildly, then called out coyly, "Need a lift, pretty lady?"

Dominick, her driver, came around and opened up the door for me.

"Is this a magic Escalade?" I asked her, climbing in and buckling up. "How did you get here so fast? It's like you have a radar for when I'm going to need you to bail me out of some disaster."

"How many times do I have to remind you of my psychic power?" SBB laughed. "Oh no," she said, grabbing my arm. "You got what appears to be marinara on your cute new-old skirt."

I looked down at the large red smudge on my Beacon's Closet skirt and said, "Ugh. Least of my worries."

SBB stuck up her pointer finger. "But the most easily fixable," she said as she started to rummage through a giant Scoop shopping bag. "I bought my yearly supply of Hanky Panky's this afternoon, and when I was at the register, I saw this fabulous skirt that just screamed 'Buy me for Flan.' So I did!"

After pulling out a few pairs of tiny seamless thong underwear, SBB produced a short green pleated Diane Samandi skirt that did, in fact, scream Flan Flood.

"Wow, thanks, SBB," I said. "I'm so glad you listened to your inner voice."

"Me, too!" she grinned. "Because do you know what else my inner voice told me today?"

I shook my head and found myself staring at a giant deep blue diamond ring on SBB's right pinky finger. "Um, 'Put in the winning bid for the Hope Diamond?'" I said, seizing her hand and gaping at her.

"Oh, this?" she said, blushing and clutching the ring to her heart. "It was a gift."

"Jake Riverdale gave you this rock, SBB? It's the size of Delaware!"

"We had a tiff. He wanted to make nice. He said not to let the paparazzi see me with it on so they won't make a fuss, but *I* plan—wait, I'm getting distracted. I wanted to tell you what else my inner voice told me to do tonight."

I nodded for her to go on.

"Dominick," she called into a speaker on the console of the back seat. "We're ready."

Through the glass pane separating the front seat from the back, Dominick passed back a familiar-looking white paper bag that I quickly realized came from one of my favorite places on earth.

"Is that what I think it is?" I asked.

"Duh. I was making my daily run to Pinkberry and my inner voice told me to pick up an extra order for you as a 'Welcome back to school' treat. I was going to call you and run it over on my way home, but then you beat me to it." She passed over one tub of the frozen yogurt to me. "Cheers!"

As we dug into our green tea fro-yos topped with raspberries and Cap'n Crunch cereal, I decided to commiserate with SBB about the minor horrors of my day. By the time we'd wound our way through the downtown maze of traffic I'd finished my story, and SBB was nodding empathetically.

"Okay, here's what we do," she said. "Divide these

issues and conquer. Pizza on the skirt—taken care of. The small embarrassment of the slip 'n' fall—everyone will have forgotten it by tomorrow . . . or least by next week. And props to you for being cool about it and not playing into their bitchy games. I sense some major karma bonus points for you there. Lots of people would have come back at Willa with an extra-large margherita pizza in the face." She waved her spoon at me. "Next, the TZ-Kennedy thing. . . . Well, that's tricky. I'm going to need some time to think on that one. But as for your English class catastrophe—how about you just . . . abandon thy fear!"

"But how?" I asked. "Is it really as easy as 'abandon thy fear'? I felt like a total idiot today, and what I *fear* is being a repeat offender of the crime of stupidity."

"Not when you've got a friend like me," SBB said, throwing her arms in the air and narrowly missing the ceiling. When she saw the confused look on my face she said, "Don't tell me you've forgotten so quickly? *Loan Shark of Venice Beach*? My steamy make-out scene with Penn? I'm basically a Shakespearean scholar."

I laughed. "Actually, I think I was picturing your steamy make-out scene a little too much today. It sort of took up all my brain power and prevented me from remembering the plot."

SBB closed her eyes and smiled. "Mmm, yes, I know that feeling when it comes to thinking about Penn." She opened one eye, a trademark SBB move. "Don't ever tell Jake I said that!"

I put my hands over my heart before eating another spoonful of yogurt. "Your secret's safe with me."

"Phew. Okay. So listen, we'll tackle this Shakespeare stuff together. Oh my God, imagine me as someone's tutor! I've always wanted to play that role, all serious and academic and maybe wearing really severe glasses and a tweed blazer. For some reason, no one's ever cast me . . ."

She trailed off, and I realized that we were pulling up to my brownstone. As the Escalade slowed to a stop, SBB flung her arms out again and squealed.

"Oh my God, I almost completely forgot something of the utmost importance."

I laughed—with SBB, this could mean anything from "I need a liver transplant" to "Built by Wendy is having a sale."

"What's up?" I asked.

SBB peered into my eyes seriously and said, "I've have to go to the premiere of Jake's new film at the Paris Theatre next Thursday night, and I'm *panicked*."

"Why?" I said. "It sounds like a blast. After all, the whole world's been waiting for the premiere of *Derelict Dudes*," I teased.

"I know, I know," SBB said, missing my joke about JR's upcoming Monster Truck movie. Then with a shudder, she said, "But *she's* going to be there and you know how I get."

I knew *she* referred to SBB's nemesis, Ashleigh Ann Martin, and I knew *how I get* referred to the total freak-outs SBB had anytime she was forced to share the same red carpet as AAM.

"So." SBB clasped her hands around mine. "Can I reserve you for the night? I have this awful premonition that AAM is going to pull a Kennedy and sabotage me. She's all about wardrobe warfare, but I'm onto her! I will not show up in the same outfit as that brain cell–challenged, rehabbing—"

"Do you need me to wait in the limo with a change of clothes, just in case?" I filled in.

SBB bobbed her head gratefully. "You're the best, Flannie. Now let's say goodnight in Shakespearean," she coached.

"Um," I said, racking my brain. "Parting is such sweet sorrow?"

"Exactly!" SBB clucked her tongue. "My first student—and she's learning so fast!"

As the Escalade started to pull away, SBB called out, "Don't forget about Thursday! Put it in the neutralizing magnetic Teslar day planner I bought you for Christmas!"

"I'm all yours," I called back.

Just as I got inside my house, I felt my phone buzz inside my bag.

IF YOU'RE GOING TO FALL DOWN IN THIS CITY, I KNOW A MUCH BETTER PLACE TO DO IT. HOW ABOUT ICE SKATING AT WOLLMAN RINK WEDNESDAY AFTER SCHOOL. —ALEX

I felt a grin spread across my face. Hmm . . . wardrobe backup with SBB next Thursday, ice skating with Alex Wednesday. Looked like I'd be getting some use out of that Teslar day planner already.

Chapter 8

The next morning, I woke up feeling a little bit more in the swing of things. I didn't short-circuit the toaster oven, so I actually got to have breakfast. I left on time and found a cab right on Perry Street, so I didn't have to book it to make the bell. And the sun was out, which made the cold air and brisk wind a whole lot more bearable.

But the best part of the morning was that when I walked into the library for study hall, I immediately honed in on the third table, and just like Camille had said, it was crammed with all my friends.

Camille stuck her arm in the air to wave. As I made my way toward the table, I realized that I already recognized a lot more faces than I had only yesterday.

"Hey, girl," Olivia called out to me from one of the computer stations as I walked past. "Let's grab coffee sometime this week."

"Totally," I whispered back, noticing that the librarian was giving me the squint eye from behind her bifocals. "I'll text you, okay?"

At the next table, Ramsey was going over a math problem with a towheaded girl in a white Oxford shirt and a black cashmere vest. When she saw me walk past, she pointed her finger and said, "This is the Stuy transfer I was telling you about. We're on for practice tonight, right, Flan?"

"Totally," I nodded. "Can't wait."

Ramsey gave me a thumbs up. I returned the gesture, crossing my fingers that she didn't expect me to be some great, untapped field hockey talent just because I came from a school where other people played it well.

I was just about to sit down next to Camille when I felt a tap on my shoulder. I turned around to find Shira Riley grinning at me. Shira was one of the most popular girls in the senior class. Camille had told me that she was suspended for a week this past fall after the dean got wind of Shira's role as ringleader in the underclassmen hazing that went down during the traditional Thoney initiation the first week of school. She had a perfect body, hair that most girls had to pay hundreds of dollars for in Japanese straightening treatments, giant brown eyes . . . and just a little bit of a history with my brother, Patch.

"Hi, Shira," I said.

Standing in my living room eating ice cream with Patch, Shira had always seemed pretty cool to me. But standing here in the middle of the Thoney library with its unspoken social seating and the darting eyes of a hundred other girls, Shira looked every bit the part of Queen Bee.

"Hey, Flan," she said, and then reached out in a surprise move to give me a big hug. I could almost hear the other freshmen girls around me gasp.

"Patch called me yesterday and told me that his little sis was starting up at Thoney. He made me promise to look out for you and make sure you're settling in okay."

For a second, I was surprised that Patch had called all the way from Croatia. But then, it would be like him to make sure there were reinforcements to look after me when he wasn't around to do it himself.

"Yeah, he was on a train to Sarajevo," she continued. "I don't know how he gets away with missing so much school! But the two of us should definitely join in on his spring break plans."

"Totally," I said, a little breathless.

"Fabulous." Shira grinned and flounced back down the aisle toward the upperclassmen tables.

I took a seat between Camille and Harper, aware that many eyes were still on me after my tête-à-tête with Shira.

"Um, did Shira Riley just *hug* you?" Amory whispered over the top of her white fluffy Rebecca Beeson turtleneck sweater.

"Yeah," I said, trying to sound like I hadn't been totally caught off-guard myself. "She went on a couple of dates with my brother."

Harper's jaw dropped. She leaned over the mahogany table and hissed, "She blindfolded Anna Jacobs and made her stick her hand in the toilet to touch a peeled banana during Freshman Haze Week."

Camille busted out laughing. "Omigod, is *that* why she got suspended? What a lame trick."

"Kind of," Harper said, but she was laughing, too. "I'm still scared of her."

I cocked my head and looked at the table where Shira was sitting with her friends. Sure, they looked really cool and put-together, but they also looked like us, just a group of friends sitting around a table, laughing about some inside joke no one else in the world would find funny. I couldn't imagine myself ever hazing any underclassmen, but I did get this weird momentary glimpse into the future—that in three more years, our table in the library might be one that looked just as intimidating to a group of new freshmen girls.

"She's not so bad, you guys, really," I said. "Patch told her to look out for me. She said to let her know if there's anything I need."

"Anything at all?" Camille asked, rubbing her chin and looking mischievous. "Why don't you ask her to make Willa stick her hand in a toilet?"

That mental image sent our whole table into hysterics, and we could barely pull it together even when the librarian came over with her finger over her lips to hiss us into silence.

When we'd finally quieted down and even opened a textbook or two, I looked up to see Mattie standing at the head of our table with a handful of square purple envelopes in her hand.

"Special delivery from the Student Senate," she said, handing out heavy calligraphed envelopes to each of us.

"Ooh, do you think this is for the January Virgil?" Morgan asked, as Mattie turned on her heel and went on her way, distributing the envelopes to the rest of the girls in the library.

All five of us opened our envelopes and pulled out

slate gray invitations with cream colored ribbon tied to the top. An iridescent opal font spelled out the details of the first Virgil party of the semester, which would take place at the Central Park Boathouse a week from this Friday.

"Wait a second," I said. "Virgil? Is this that oration challenge thing Thoney does with the Dalton boys?"

"Whoa," Camille said. "Pulling out the Thoney tradition trivia. Did you get that from some old story Mama Flood told you about her days as a private school girl?

Harper folded her hands primly and put on her best debating voice. "Virgil *used* to be a night of debates between the guys and the girls. Everyone got all decked out and riled up to argue with each other. It was hot."

"So hot," Camille said, teasing Harper about her obsession with all things debate.

"But somewhere along the way," Harper continued unaware, "the actual debating sorta fell by the wayside. What we do at Virgil now is—"

"Drink cocktails!" Morgan and Amory chimed in at the same time.

"*Virgin* cocktails," Harper corrected. "But it's totally swanky and fun."

"And the best part is," Camille said, "one Thoney

girl gets to be the social director for each Virgil event." She looked down at the invitation and read, "Nominations will take place this week, and the host will be announced on Monday."

"And being host is a good thing?" I said, watching other clusters of freshmen around us whispering excitedly over their invites.

"It's, like, the hugest honor there is," Harper said, looking serious.

"You're basically Miss Thoney of the month," Morgan said, barely looking up as she flipped through *The Pulse* magazine.

"Flan," Amory said, "you should totally run. You're the new girl, which makes you the ingénue. You have this air of mystique about you, and everyone will want to get to know you. This will be a great way for you to solidify yourself on the Thoney scene."

"I don't know," I said. "Wouldn't people rather vote for someone they know?" Hosting sounded like a lot of work. I'd planned some really fun parties in my day, but I was also totally down with being the girl who just showed up and had an amazing time.

Amory cleared her throat and nodded her head toward two tables over where Willa was sitting with Kennedy. "You mean like Willa? Queen Bitch over there is class president and *thinks* she's going to win, but I personally *will not* be voting for her."

"I second that motion!" Harper added, banging her Paul Frank glasses case down on the table like a gavel.

The rest of us covered our mouths with our hands to keep from laughing so we wouldn't get kicked out of the library by the already pissed-off Miss Dorsey.

As it turned out, the librarian may have been too engrossed in her microfiche to bother with us at the moment . . . but someone else had taken a particular interest in our conversation.

In her purple Vera Wang turtleneck wrap dress, Willa nudged Kennedy and the two of them looked up and glared at us.

"Yow," Camille whispered to me. "If looks could kill, I'd be writing your eulogy right now."

Before I could respond, Willa held up her Virgil invitation as if it were a challenge and mouthed three terrifying words.

Bring it on.

Chapter 9

After school, Camille and I swapped our skirts and Missoni sweaters for grubby sweatshirts, warm leggings, and field hockey skirts. We met up with Ramsey on the front steps of Thoney.

"Let's talk formations," Ramsey said as she started walking, very briskly, toward the river. She had an enormous mesh equipment bag slung over her shoulder, and in her red Adidas track suit and white earmuffs she looked vaguely like a version of Mrs. Claus on steroids.

"Formations?" Camille said. She practically had to break into a jog to keep up with Ramsey.

I had to give Camille major fist bumps for jumping onto the field hockey team just because she knew I'd need a friend by my side. This was just what I'd always loved about Camille. She'd try anything once, she

73

wasn't afraid to screw up, and she never, ever complained.

Still, if our early days playing Little League T-ball on the Rockettes back in third grade were any indication, I was guessing Camille wasn't exactly going to be the star forward of the team. I remembered the day our coach had decided to move the team up to a more competitive league—he called Camille's mom to politely suggest that Camille retire her purple and green uniform (complete with elbow and knee pads for all the sliding we did) and trade in T-ball for something less active, like piano.

Sure, Camille had been heartbroken for about an hour—after all, every single one of our friends played on the team, and she didn't want to be kicked out of the party. But as we sat on the tire swing near 68th Street in Central Park and moaned about how awful life was, Camille came up with an idea. She didn't have to trade in her Rockettes uniform at all. She'd just be our cheerleader.

From that day on, I've never stopped being impressed by how good a sport Camille really is, regardless of whether she was winning, losing, or completely banned from the team.

"Okay," Ramsey said. "So the first thing you have

to learn is: Defense is not the only thing. It's every-thing, except for offense. Get it?"

I was hoping that getting banned from the Thoney field hockey team wasn't anywhere in Camille's future, but as I listened to Ramsey spit out strategic sound bites, I noticed the panic in Camille's eyes and made a mental note to help her out on the field as much as I possibly could.

"It's a bummer we don't have enough girls to even get a real scrimmage going," Ramsey said. "Usually we do a lot of two-on-two exercises, just to get a feel for some of the plays."

"Great," Camille muttered to me under her breath as we fell a couple steps behind Ramsey. "I can just see it now—you and me pitted against Kennedy and Willa."

"Totally," I shuddered. "I just hope Ramsey's got extra shinguards in her bag o' fun up there."

"What's that?" Ramsey turned around. "You girls need shin guards?"

Camille and I started laughing. "Oh no," I said. "I was just making a joke. It's not a big deal."

"But it is," Ramsey said, looking serious. "A team like Stuyvesant would take one look at us with this equipment and think we don't have dedication or people at our school who truly care about our sport." She hung her head as we turned downtown at the East River. Camille and I followed her toward 90th Street and wondered what to say to lighten the mood.

"We were supposed to get this donation from the Morphew Fund over break," Ramsey went on. "It was going to cover all the gear and replace our grub uniforms, but at the last minute, the money didn't come through." Ramsey sighed and rummaged through the bag. "It looks like we're stuck with what we have for now, which is one-and-a-half pairs of shin guards. Which one of you wants 'em?"

Camille and I looked at each other. Was she asking which one of us was the easier target?

"Give them to Flan," Camille said. "Who am I kidding? I'm more of a 'Run around the sidelines' girl myself."

By then we'd passed the only field I knew of this far up on the Upper East Side, and Ramsey didn't show any signs of slowing down. I turned to Camille.

"Do you have any idea where we're going?"

Camille shook her head.

Just then, Ramsey swung a left onto a huge barge, which I quickly realized was covered in Astroturf.

"Whoa," Camille said. "Does anyone else feel like

Roger Federer playing on top of that helicopter landing pad in Dubai?"

The "field" jutted out into the East River, and as we walked out to center court, I could see the teeming Triborough Bridge to my left and the giant Coca-Cola sign across the river in Long Island City to my right. New uniforms or not, this was a pretty prime spot to play field hockey.

And apparently, we weren't the only ones enjoying the view. No sooner had the three of us tossed our bags down on the sidelines than I noticed a small crowd of familiar faces tossing a Frisbee right behind us.

"Omigod," Camille gasped. "*What* is Xander doing here? My defense is so not cute."

"First of all," I told her, "he *already* thinks your defense is cute. Second of all, I don't know what he's doing here, but whatever it is," I said, scanning the sidelines, "he's doing it with Rob."

"And Danny," Camille added, giggling when we saw Danny leap dramatically into the air to catch a Frisbee he could have easily caught by just standing there.

"And Alex," I said as we watched him jog over to meet the other guys. "What are they *doing* here?"

"And TZ," a nasty voice said from behind us.

Kennedy and her scary sidekick were both in matching Burberry field hockey getups. "And since you asked," Kennedy continued, "they're here because TZ is my boyfriend, and he understands how important it is to support my extracurriculars."

"Does he also support your extra-bitchy attitude?" Camille asked.

"Ha ha," Kennedy barked, hands on her hips.

"Okay, girls," Ramsey shouted, clearly oblivious to the drama she was interrupting. "Let's huddle up and get going."

At first, a few of the other girls on the team seemed to defer to Willa and Kennedy, but once Ramsey started leading warm-ups, it was clear she was the leader. Even without the right equipment, and even with the bad juju between the players on her team, Ramsey managed to run a pretty tight ship. We did sprints up and down the field, squats, push-ups, and then what I thought might be a never-ending set of jumping jacks. By the time we'd finished warming up, I was so tired I'd almost forgotten we had an audience.

Almost, but not quite.

It was so obvious that all the girls were consumed by not wanting to look awkward and unathletic in front of the boys. The only thing more obvious was that the Frisbee the boys had brought with them was just a decoy so they could watch us all run around the increasingly windy field in skirts.

And sure enough, Camille was a little klutzy. She tripped over her own feet a couple times, and each time, I'd glance over at Xander to see what his reaction was. Willa may have been snickering, but the look on Xander's face was so genuinely concerned that I knew Camille could fall a hundred times, and he would only find her more and more adorable.

When we split into two-on-two scrimmages, Ramsey paired Camille and me up with Willa and Kennedy. At first, it made me a little nervous, but once I got going, I realized that all that time I'd spent playing roller hockey with Patch during the summer wasn't for nothing, and that I was actually pretty good at this whole field hockey thing.

"Flan, you are totally kicking butt out there," Ramsey called out to me, and I couldn't help but look over to see whether maybe Alex had heard. Our eyes met and he gave me a thumbs-up.

Wham!

Something hard and cold had collided with my shoulder. It was Willa's bony body edging past me toward the goal.

"Way to have your eyes on the prize, Flood," she

called out, her long blond ponytail blowing in the wind.

"Hey," Ramsey said, jogging over to the spot where I'd landed on the ground. She put her arm on my shoulder, and I thought about what a great coach she'd make someday. "Listen," she said, "Willa's tough on the field, and I'm not saying everyone should play like her. But it doesn't hurt to have a couple of offensive plays up your sleeve." I knew Ramsey was all about the sport and not at all invested in the social drama going down, but I figured any little offensive tip could help. "Let me show you how to hip check," she said.

Ramsey positioned herself in front of me, and as I dribbled the ball past her, she lightly bumped my hip with hers and used her momentum to gain possession of the ball.

"Hey," I called, "nice play."

Once I got it down, I was eager to try out my new offensive moves on Willa and on Kennedy. Luckily, I didn't have to wait too long.

The next time I got the ball, both of them were on me like glue. While Camille lagged behind, I could feel them both narrowing in on me—Kennedy implementing her powerful death glare on my right, Willa baring her designer orthodontic fangs on my left.

And to think—all this time, I'd been under the impression that the games at Stuyvesant were intense. I felt myself moving faster and even sort of *growling*. Hopefully in a cute way, but still, I was deeply into it.

Sticks flashed, ponytails flipped, and our three sets of cleats pounded down the field. I didn't know how much longer I could keep dribbling the ball under this sort of pressure when suddenly, without thinking, I tried out the double hip check.

"Oww!" Kennedy bellowed.

"Argh," Willa growled, and amazingly, my one-two punch knocked both of them out of my field of view. Before I knew it, I'd blown past them, and I went on to score the goal.

When I looked behind me, Kennedy was fuming. She definitely wasn't a pretty sight when she was angry. Seeing her all red-faced and panting made me wonder—not for the first time—what it was exactly that TZ saw in her.

But I had to admit: It was pretty amazing to see her so riled up. Now all I had to do was figure out how to do it *off* the field.

I expected to see Willa at Kennedy's side, plotting their next attack against me, but Kennedy was picking the grass off her skirt alone, and Willa was nowhere to be seen. Finally, I spotted her crouched on the ground, groaning and clutching her side. Whoops. I guess maybe I hip checked her a little harder than I'd meant to. I jogged toward her to make sure she was all right.

"Willa," I said, leaning down. "Are you okay? I'm sorry. I didn't mean for things to get so rough."

I stuck out my hand to help her up. She stared at it for a moment like I was offering her some kind of contagious disease.

"Well gee, thanks, Flan," she said, deciding in the end to take my hand. She put away the fangs for a change and gave me a sugary sweet smile as she stood up.

From the other side of the field, to the boys or to Ramsey it might have looked like we were just two teammates helping each other out. But when Willa got to her feet, I felt the hard grind of her cleat dig into my toe.

"Oww." I pulled my foot back and tried to do the same with my hand, but she just squeezed it tighter.

"Can I just say one thing?" she asked, her voice still dripping saccharine. "That whole running-for-host thing that your little friends are trying to put you up to"—she clucked her tongue—"so not a good idea. You see, there's an order to what happens at this school." She finally released my hand and took a step away from me. "It's like this: Everyone knows that I'm in line to be this Virgil Host. Hardly anyone even knows who you are. And if I were you, Flood, I'd keep it that way."

$\mathcal{J}$ was so shell-shocked (and hip sore) by Willa's utter scariness on the field that I nearly forgot that night was my monthly "Cheap Thai food and trashy movie night" with SBB. We'd started the tradition when SBB was in a slump over some bad press she'd gotten for *Willow Walks with Wendy*, a cheesy date movie she'd starred in with the fallen former child star Fenton McCallister.

When the movie debuted, I'd spent days trying to convince SBB that even though the *New York Post* had called it "horrifyingly vapid," that her own acting had been much more highly praised (relatively speaking) as "borderline inoffensive." But the only thing that seemed to cheer SBB up in those days was to watch movies that she claimed were worse than *Willow Walks*.

Somewhere along the way, bad movies and pad thai

became a tradition. Now that we'd seen just about every Keanu Reeves movie in existence, it was almost a challenge to keep digging up disasters that would beat the one we'd watched the month before. But somehow, we always found one.

By the time SBB rang my doorbell, I was stretched out on the couch with a heating pad slung over my hip.

"Door's open," I called out. "I'm infirm and can't get up."

SBB stepped into my living room wearing a geometric print bodysuit, bobby socks, and a high black babushka. More often than not, I wanted to crack up when SBB showed up at my house wearing something ridiculous. But I always had to remember to keep myself in check. If she was wearing it today, everyone on the street would almost certainly be wearing a toned-down version of it next month. Though in this case, I doubted very many people on the street could pull off a geometric print bodysuit. But a New Yorker could always try.

"Grub's here!" she called out, holding up a large paper bag that was filling the room with some very tantalizing smells. "And I brought *Joe Versus the Volcano*."

Then, when she got a glimpse of my position on the

couch, SBB dropped the bag and darted over to me. "Oh my God, what happened to you? Don't tell me you got in a catfight with Kennedy?" She surveyed my face. "At least she didn't give you a black eye."

"It wasn't exactly a catfight," I said. "And it wasn't exactly with Kennedy."

"Flan, you're scaring me. Since when do you get into full-on brawls with unknown Manhattanites?"

"Since I joined the field hockey team this afternoon. It just got a little bit, um, aggressive. And it was Kennedy's best friend-slash-Satan, Willa. The two of us were a smidge too into the hip checking. Don't worry, though, I'll recover."

SBB was still stuck on one thing. "Willa Rubenstein?" she asked, eyes wide. "*That cow.*"

I shook my head. "No, she's tiny. Too tiny to contain all that scariness, actually."

"Well she didn't used to be," SBB said, busily unloading the tubs of Thai food from the bag now that she'd been assured that my condition wasn't life-threatening.

"What do you mean?" I asked.

SBB sat poised on the arm of the couch. "Back when her mother had fooled herself and a couple of agents from ACA into thinking Willa had a chance as an actor, we used to audition together. Willa always tried out for the chubby girl parts. And I'm pretty sure her dad even went so far as to pay off the casting crew just so she could try out. I think she did a commercial or two. But then that was it. *Over*." SBB shook her head.

"Well, she's skinny now," I said, spooling some noodles and broccoli around my chopsticks. "And completely evil. I don't get it. You know, at least Kennedy and I have a history. We have a reason not to get along. Willa just seems to get a kick out of being nasty to someone she barely knows."

SBB dipped a spring roll into some peanut sauce and took a giant bite. "Maybe she's threatened by you," she said with her mouth full.

"Yeah, right," I said. "Class president, totally put-together, richest girl in school. There's no way she'd be threatened by me. I'm the new girl who trips into whole pizzas, remember?"

"The new girl who trips into whole pizzas and can bounce back, stand up, and laugh about it. Don't underestimate yourself, Flan," she said. "Clearly you have something that Willa wants."

I considered this. "She wants me not to run for Virgil Host. She made that pretty clear today," I said, lifting up the heating pad to check on my hip. "I have the bruises to prove it."

"Well," SBB said with a knowing look. "If Willa doesn't want you to run, then obviously you have to run. And not only that, you have to *win*. What is this Virgil Host thing, anyway?"

I shrugged. "It's sort of like the party planner of the month. You basically arrange a swanky event with Dalton. And get this, there's an actual election to decide who's most qualified for the job."

"Well, if Willa's so bitchy, who's even going to vote for her?" SBB said. "You've already got a leg up on her just by being a nice person."

I shook my head. "I don't know if it's about niceness at Thoney."

"Everybody likes niceness," SBB said.

In SBB's movie version of my life, maybe this was true. Unfortunately, it didn't look like real life followed the same script.

"Not on the Upper East Side. It's so cutthroat. Sometimes I can't believe how ridiculous the code of conduct is at this school."

SBB put her hand up to stop me. "I usually don't talk with my mouth full, Flan, but I need to interrupt you. It may be ridiculous to have to run for such an office, but this title sounds like it was made for you."

"No way."

"Yes way," SBB said. "I'm still picking confetti off

my clothes from the birthday party you threw me. You're the best party planner I know."

"That was a pretty sweet party," I said, thinking back to the two hundred balloons we'd floated on the pool at the Q hotel in Midtown for SBB's last birthday. "But I'm not sure I could actually *campaign* for my party planning skills. It sounds a little intense."

Before I could argue any further, the front door of our house burst open and in pranced Feb with the wispiest, pixiest-looking girl I'd ever seen. Both of them were dressed entirely in black, and Feb had my Pomeranian, Noodles, cradled in a small tote bag under her arm.

"Noodles!" I practically shrieked. "Thank God—I was wondering where you were!"

"Sorry, Flan, I sent you a text when we got back from Cambodia. I had to borrow him for an hour. It's just so French to port around a little pooch, *n'est-ce pas?*"

"Huh?" SBB and I said at the same time.

Feb gestured at the bob-headed pixie to her left. "This is Jade Moodswing. This is my sister, Flan, and her actress friend, Sara-Beth Benny."

"Is pleasure to meet you," Jade said in a thick French accent. Her mauve-penciled lips were set in a deep frown as she began to move around the room, picking up my mom's vases, clocks, and candlesticks.

She gave everything a very discerning once over. Then, with exquisite ladylike elegance, she took a seat next to me on the couch and crossed one leg over the other like she was in a French spy film from the forties. She took a cigarette out of a slim silver case, looked around, seemed to think better of lighting it in our living room, replaced the cigarette, and sighed heavily, like she just remembered every boy she'd had to break up with since she was seven years old, and it was all too much to handle. I'd never seen someone look so beautiful while brooding before. It was more than a little bit mesmerizing.

"So what brings you to New York?" I asked her.

"*Pff.*" Jade puffed a breath of air out of her lips. "Always work. But your sister is helping me plan my fashion show at The Armory Show. In fact—" She looked me up and down in the same way she'd just examined our Nambé candlesticks. Then, without hesitation, she reached forward and ran her thumb along my cheekbones. Normally, I might have jumped back at a virtual stranger doing that, but something about Jade doing it made me feel honored. Even if I had absolutely no idea what she was doing.

She clapped her hands. "February," she said, strongly pronouncing the first *r*. "I wonder if we have just found our model?"

"Huh?" Now Feb, SBB, and I all spoke at the same time.

Jade nodded as if whatever she was talking about had already been decided. "Your sister, she is . . . how do you say . . . so fetching, youthful, long-legged. *Très Américaine. J'adore.*"

Suddenly, I heard a low rumbling purr sound. Confused, I looked around for a cat before I realized we didn't have one—and then I figured out that the sound was coming from Jade. I could feel myself blushing when I said, "Seriously? Me?"

"It's not actually the most horrible idea in the world," Feb said. She whipped out her iPhone, took a picture of me, then passed the phone to Jade, who proceeded to get up off the couch and play paparazzi. After a minute, they drifted out of the room, conferring over the photos.

To my right, I heard a *hmph!* and looked over to see SBB with her arms crossed over her chest like a pouting three-year-old.

"What's that face?" I asked her, tucking my knees under my chin.

"Nothing," she sniffed, looking at the ceiling. Noodles jumped into her lap and licked her chin. "What face?"

"*SBB.*" I said. "What's wrong?"

SBB swept Noodles's poofy fur into a spiky pony-tail between his ears. "*I've* been trying to get you to do fashion for years. Now some *étrangère* rushes in with the idea and suddenly you're intrigued?"

It was just like SBB to get possessive over me at a moment like this, and I had to remind myself that this was just her funny way of showing that she cared. As long as she could be included, SBB was my biggest supporter, no matter what I did.

"I don't even know if I'm intrigued," I said as SBB gave Noodles another ponytail. He licked her again, then jumped off the couch.

"You blushed, and I know what that means. That you're sitting there thinking *ooh la la*, a French designer, an *artiste*, who is so fancy and French and way better at fashion than SBB."

"SBB—never! You are the most stylish person I know." I swatted her arm playfully. "But it's a little interesting sounding, I guess. It's just that I'm not quite feeling comfortable yet at school, and maybe doing this modeling gig would be a distraction. Do you think it's a bad idea?" I asked.

Feeling needed once again, SBB instantly changed her tune. She cocked her head to one side and looked like she was thinking hard. "You know what," she said after a pause, "if you're looking for a way to feel more accustomed to your new school . . . a French fashion show at The Armory Show is totally Park Avenue. It's so Uptown. It's *sooo* Thoney." She grinned at me. "*And* I'm guessing it's something even Willa's daddy can't buy for her. Think how absolutely green with envy she'll be," she trilled, hugging a French silk pillow to her chest.

SBB did have a point. It would be exactly the kind of thing that everyone at Thoney would find pretty impressive. And I wondered, if I started hanging out with Jade Moodswing a little bit, whether some of her cool Moodswing-ness might rub off on me. There was something about this that sounded strangely appealing.

"I love black currant tea in glass tumbler," Jade said as she drifted back into the room. "So, Flan, have you decided? Feb and I think you should say *oui*."

Feb brushed a tuft of dog fur off her dress. "You know how much I love a family affair," she said with a wink in my direction, which was code for "You know how much I love the chance to boss my little sister around."

"It does sound fun," I said timidly. "But can I take a few days to think about it and let you know?" As intrigued as I was, I knew modeling was so not my turf. I was the girl who skinned her knee rollerblading along Chelsea Piers the week before. Tonight I got totally down and dirty on a field hockey court. I tripped over pizzas for God's sake. How could I be expected to handle a catwalk?

But Jade just shook her head. "I knew I would find my model today. *Voilà*, it is settled. Now, Flan, will you get me more tea? I like it very much boiling, please."

*B*y my third day at Thoney, I was finally getting the hang of things. English was scaring me less and less, and I could navigate the hallways without the use of Camille's rumpled napkin map. Even the social "rules" of the first day of school were starting to feel a little bit more natural, mostly because I realized that I didn't have to let them stop me from being myself. After all, I had to remind myself, being myself was fun.

It was only lunchtime and I'd already succeeded in helping a sophomore girl pick up her dropped books in the stairwell, complimented Olivia on her awesome feather headband when I passed her in the courtyard, and made a girl named Faiden's day when I told her in social studies that I'd always wanted to name my daughter Faiden.

Not that I was tallying my niceness points or

anything, but maybe SBB was right. Maybe there was something to just being a good person. Maybe I *could* use my personality to my advantage and secure this Virgil Host thing. Hmm . . .

When I got to the cafeteria, I took a quick glimpse at the menu offerings and remembered right away that the mac and cheese and the fries had been pre-approved by Camille.

I grabbed a bottle of green tea and an order of the mac and cheese and decided to take a last-minute gamble on the split pea soup. At the register, a girl behind me with giant plastic earrings shaped like rosebuds was eyeing my tray.

"Sometimes I think if I have to eat another fry," she said, "I'll turn into a potato." She laughed and shook her head. "It's stupid, but I'm scared to branch out—is that soup any good?"

"I haven't tried it yet," I told her, counting out change from my Lancel wallet. "I'll let you know, though. The mac and cheese is always a safe bet, too."

The girl nodded emphatically, like I'd said something really insightful. "Thanks," she said, lifting a serving of the cheesy pasta off the lineup of mostly scary-looking foods.

"No problem." I smiled and made my way to the third table where my friends were waiting, wondering:

What Would Willa Have Done? Probably tripped Plastic Earrings and laughed.

"Hey, Flan," a voice called out as I walked to my table. I looked over and was kind of excited to find that the speaker was one of Shira Riley's senior friends.

"Hi, Anna," I said, noticing that she was sporting the same Comptoir des Cotonniers satchel that Jade Moodswing had had with her last night. "Cool bag," I said, feeling a little impressed with myself that I recognized the French designer. "I love their new line."

"Me, too," Anna said, nudging Shira, who was sitting behind her. "Looks like Patch's little sister has some taste."

As I walked past them, I started thinking about how long it had been since someone referred to me as "Patch's little sister." There was a time when it used to bug me, like I wasn't my own person. In fact, I think Patch's shadow was a big part of the reason why I wanted to try out Stuyvesant. But now that I had that experience under my belt, I'd learned a couple of key things. For starters, I knew I was my own person—and I also knew that whatever fashion sense I did have definitely did *not* come from my wrinkled T-shirt-wearing brother.

Finally, I spotted Camille, Harper, Morgan, and

Amory and gave them all a big smile. Even though the cafeteria was a flurry of activity—Bill Blass heels clicking, cell phones ringing, and one very insane-looking janitor gathering all the soda cans out of the trash bins and muttering to himself about who knows what—the third table felt like a total mecca of serenity. It was so great to know that I had thirty-five blissful minutes to just relax with my friends and chow down.

"How's it going, girls?" I said, plopping down in an empty seat next to Camille. Harper was dusting her eyes with gold shimmer, Morgan was tapping a beat with her fork on the table, and Amory was memorizing her monologue for the upcoming play tryouts.

"Well, I'm basically in awe watching you, Flan," Camille said, shaking her head. "Here you were, all nervous about coming back to private school, and within three days, it's like you already know everyone."

"I guess I'm just starting to feel more comfortable." I shrugged.

Morgan put her fork down and laughed. "And is this newfound comfort making you bold enough to try the cafeteria soup? You just might be the bravest girl in this room."

To show off my alleged bravery, I dunked my spoon into the mysteriously green soup and brought it to my lips.

"Actually," I said, "it's pretty good. Anyone want to try?"

The soup was passed around the table and voted unanimously acceptable.

"She's in with the senior girls," Camille listed on her hand. "She's expanding our horizons at the lunch line. What's next, Flan?"

Harper looked up from her Stila compact mirror and said, "You should buy a lottery ticket. This seems like your lucky week."

"Actually," I said, "I was sort of thinking about what you guys were saying the other day about the Virgil Host thing—"

"Ugh," Amory interjected. She looked gorgeous as usual in a cobalt blue Marc Jacobs sweater with adorable square buttons. "This morning, I was in the bathroom rehearsing my lines for auditions and I totally heard Willa proclaiming her victory. She was talking about how she wants to implement a VIP Host's table where the Host and her guests of choice will sit at—get this—an *elevated* table so they can reign over the whole event. I can just see Willa and Kennedy sitting there glowering at everyone, making judgmental comments about what people are wearing, and hoarding all the boys."

"Gag me," Harper said, rolling her eyes before

adding another coat of MAC mascara. "There's got to be a logical way to thwart Willa's evil dominion."

"Well, I started thinking about it last night," I told the girls. "You know, about how brutal she was at practice—*so* not my style, by the way—and how she thinks she owns the school. And I don't know, I guess I started thinking that maybe there are benefits to having such a different way of being in the world. If Willa thinks she can scare people into voting for her so she can lord over us at Virgil, I figure I can try the opposite approach."

"Kill them with kindness?" Camille said, digging her spoon back into my soup for another bite. A little dropped on the table, which she wiped up with her napkin.

"Exactly," I said.

"Well, I know who I'm voting for," Morgan said, sipping her Mango Kombucha tea and making a gagging face as she swallowed. "Please tell me—does anyone on earth actually *like* the way this stuff tastes? First and last time I'm buying it."

Harper put her makeup away. "What you need now is a campaign slogan," she said, pulling out a pen and a notebook to take notes. She was definitely proving to be the organized one of the bunch.

"And maybe some really hot 'Flan Rocks' T-shirts?"

Amory added. "Costume always makes the charac-ter."

"And a theme song," Morgan said, forgetting the gross Kombucha and bobbing up and down in her seat like a little kid on her way to the Bronx Zoo. "Can I please, please, please be your music coordinator?"

"Of course," I said, feeling a grin spread across my face. "I can use all the help I can get."

"Ooh," Camille said, "project! Way to step up the team effort, girls. Not that it'll be that hard to con-vince the school to love Flan even more by Monday, but it sounds like we have a busy week ahead of us."

As we finished lunch and made our way to the exit, I could tell the girls were just as excited about this campaign as I was. Sure, it sounded like it might be a lot of work—on top of keeping up with my English work and field hockey practice, and was I *really* going to do this modeling thing for Jade Moodswing?—but everyone works best under pressure, right?

"I really hope you're not busy tonight," I heard a voice say behind me just as I reached the hallway.

For a second I thought the person was talking to me, so I turned to say that I actually did have plans—skating with Alex and then meeting SBB for a shop-ping date in SoHo.

But when I realized that the voice belonged to

Willa—and that she wasn't talking to me—I quickly shut my mouth and turned back around.

"What's she up to?" Camille asked suspiciously as a small crowd gathered around Willa. Something about it made my stomach cramp up. I'd been feeling so confident during lunch, but seeing the student body hold court around Willa was a grim reminder that she definitely had some major sway at Thoney. After all, they *had* voted her class president.

"My father's screening a brand-new movie tonight at the Aphrodite," she announced prissily. "Everyone from our class is invited." Willa placed invitations one by one in the hands of her admirers. When she turned to me and my friends, she paused. "Whoops, well, *almost* everyone. Sorry, Flan. Coincidentally, I *just* ran out of invitations."

It was all so pathetically staged, but the weirdest thing was that it seemed to work. All around me, freshmen girls were opening their invitations with universal *oohs* and *aahs*. Sure, I was curious about the screening, but I wasn't going to let Willa see it get to me.

"No biggie," I told her, looking at her perfect blue eyes and trying to play it off. "I wouldn't have been able to make it anyway."

Willa leaned forward, both arms crossed over her

chest. "Wow, lying about having other plans comes so naturally to you. You must be used to being excluded. Sad." She put her finger on her chin in deep mock-thought. "Don't worry, you and your little friends can always Netflix my father's movies any Saturday night when you have nothing better to do."

I opened my mouth to come back at her, but Harper grabbed my arm. "Don't waste your breath on rebuttal right now," she said. "You'll get Willa back when it counts."

I wanted to believe she was right, but in the face of Willa's icy stare, I started to wonder whether I was really up for this. Harper might be able to teach me every trick in the debating book, but Willa was out for blood.

*L*ater that afternoon, I was standing in front of the full-length mirror in my bedroom wondering why there were never any wardrobe indecision scenes in fairy tales. I found it hard to believe that all these girls just knew what to wear to the ball with Prince Charming. Here I was, getting ready for my skating date with the Prince of New York, and feeling totally crippled by my lack of costume options.

This wasn't like me. Usually I just slapped on whatever I was most comfortable in, as per my mother's cardinal rule: In order to look comfortable in your own skin, you have to first feel comfortable in your clothes.

But now I was rifling through my closet, feeling absolutely certain that I had nothing at all to wear on this first date. I thought about popping down the street to Intermix or Marc Jacobs—but nothing I'd seen in the windows recently seemed quite right either.

Was the Thoney preppiness getting to me already?

Or was it something about Alex that was intimidating me?

I'd first met Alex in the Hamptons a few Fourth of Julys ago. It was the summer between seventh and eighth grades, when my friends and I spent our time hanging out with guys who were constantly trying to outdo each other organizing late night parties on the beach.

I remember Alex stood out because he insisted that everyone go through this one private entrance behind Garrison Toyota's mansion. People were complaining about having to sneak in, about how the view from Alex's parents' private beach was even better than the one we were risking getting busted to see. The night I met Alex, I remember Camille summing it up perfectly by saying, "This guy must just get a thrill out of breaking every rule he can find."

In a way, I sort of got that. I'd seen Alex at parties around the city after that, and I'd watched the way crowds of people parted like the Red Sea so that he could get to the front of the line to grab a drink or enter a club. He was the president of the sophomore class and the captain of the lacrosse team. Apparently, he never even studied to get the elusive Dalton A. If everything came easy for him, I could sort of see why he might have to make his own challenges.

But when I applied that theory to his interest in me, it made me more than a little bit nervous. Was it possible that Alex saw *me* as some sort of challenge?

And then . . . what would a challenge wear on a first date?

When I finally did make it out the door to meet Alex at Wollman Rink in Central Park, I'd decided on the black leggings (of Kennedy infamy) and a long dark red sweater. Not exactly fairy princess material, but it did match my new red earmuffs, and I knew it was going to be freezing on the ice.

When I got to the park a few minutes after five o'clock, Alex was leaning on the railing that looked out over the rink. Against the backdrop of Central Park South's glittering skyscrapers, in his pin-striped blazer, orange scarf, and skates slung over his shoulder, he really did look like the Prince of New York.

"Ready to get klutzy out there?" he asked with a smile. Normally, I'd turn beet red if a guy I liked teased me about something as mortifying as my pizza party foul. But when I looked at Alex, he was smiling, and all of a sudden I didn't mind what he'd said.

"You don't even know what I'm capable of on the

ice," I teased back. "Get ready to feel deeply jealous of my moves."

"Actually, I'm already a little jealous," he said, looking more serious. "You looked pretty smooth out there during field hockey practice. I guess you played on the team at Stuy?"

"Uh-uh," I said, shaking my head. "That practice you saw was my first one."

"You're kidding," he said. "You were great."

"Beginner's luck," I said, feeling a shiver as Alex touched my back to lead me down the steps to the skate rental booth.

We found a spot on the bench and Alex helped me tie up my skates. It was no glass slipper, but it still felt sort of like a fairy tale to me.

Soon, Alex had taken my hand and was pulling me out on the ice. "I've never seen this place so empty," Alex said, wrapping his arm around my waist. "It's like we have our own private rink."

It had been a long time since I'd been skating. The last time Camille and I had made the mistake of going to Rock Center pre-Christmas, there'd been less actual skating and more shuffling against a thousand other people on a tiny fleck of a rink.

Today, though, Wollman Rink was wide open. The cold must have scared off a lot of tourists and little kids. But I realized that as long as you had earmuffs and the warm hand of someone like Alex, it wasn't all that bad. In fact, as we whirled around the rink a few times to warm up, it was actually incredibly romantic.

"The most exclusive skating party in the world," I said. "And we didn't even have to sneak in through Garrison Toyota's backyard to get here." There was something about our rapport that made it easy and fun to tease each other.

"Hey—watch it there," he said, giving me a squeeze. "Speaking of exclusive, how are you finding Thoney life?"

"So far, it's been fun," I said, trying to choose the right words. "But sometimes I feel like everyone's playing a game that I didn't get the rule book for."

"I don't believe in rules." Alex shrugged. "Well, at least not the annoying ones."

"I know," I said. "And the Thoney rules are borderline ridiculous, but the girls seem to take them so seriously."

"Like what?" He rubbed his gloved hands together.

I thought about Willa's Virgil campaigning and considered whether to bring up the whole Host thing to Alex. It did sound a little lame to say it out loud, but he was looking at me so sincerely with his dark eyes that I decided to go for it. "Well, there's this . . . position I'm running for . . . to host this party—"

"Virgil?" he said. "Virgil Host is serious stuff. My older sister was super into it. You're going to run?"

"I guess so. I was kind of put up to it by my friends. But now it seems like there are all these things I have to do to win—all these favors I'm supposed to give, this whole strategy I'm supposed to follow."

Alex seemed to think about this for a minute. "Hey, remember that surprise hip check you worked on the field yesterday?" he said.

"Yeah, I still have the bruises from the aftermath," I said. "But what does that have to do with Virgil?"

Alex laughed. "Maybe you don't have to know *all* the strategies. Just pick the tricks that work for you so you can win the game." He skated forward and gave me a light bump on the hip.

"You're doing it all wrong," I said, laughing, then boldly taking a light bump back at his hip. "It's like this."

"My bad," he said, laughing too. "You know, I think you might be able to trademark that move: the Flood."

"Right. If I could just find the off-field equivalent of the hip check, then I'd totally rock the competition," I joked.

"Exactly." Alex nodded. "You'll be Virgil Host in no time."

Alex's eyes locked on mine, and he started to skate up next to me. His face was only inches away from mine, and I realized I was holding my breath.

Just then, a careening ice-skater in a giant blue puffy coat came flying into us, knocking himself—and the two of us—to the ground.

"Ouch!" I cried out when my butt hit the ice.

"You two should watch where you're going," the man called out angrily. It was hard to see his face under his Yankees ski cap, but he seemed more embarrassed than legitimately huffy. Before we could respond, he got to his feet, brushed himself off, and wobbily skated away.

"Hey, are you okay?" Alex called out.

"I think so," I said, checking myself for bruises. "I don't think I've fallen this many times in one week since I'd figured out how to walk."

When I looked over at Alex, I couldn't help but crack up. His hair was covered in snowy ice residue. "But you look like you just aged forty years."

"Oh yeah?" Alex grinned, pointing at my head. "Bold words from someone who's only got half her earmuffs on, don't you think?"

"Where'd that guy go?" I said as Alex helped me

straighten my earmuffs. "Somebody should hip check him."

"Dude, seriously," he said, looking around the rink.

"Yeah, but he was pretty big. I nominate you."

Alex laughed and held up his hands. "Not it."

"Hey, you're supposed to be chivalrous and protect me," I joked.

"Wait a minute. I thought you were the pro-hip checker. Why don't you show everyone here how it's done?"

By then the puffy-jacketed problem skater was nowhere to be found. But the sun was setting over Central Park West, and I realized I was having way too much fun with Alex to care.

*D*owntown a few hours later, I fell into a whole other kind of intense experience: a shopping date with SBB. When I met her at Nanette Lepore on Broome Street, my head may still have been twirling around Wollman Rink with Alex. But soon enough, my body was being twirled around the hot pink-painted floors of the evening wear section of the boutique by one very riled-up starlet.

"Flan! Thank *God* you're here," she gasped when the door chime jingled to announce my arrival. "Can you *believe* it's less than eight days until the premiere, and I still have nothing to wear?" She clutched her phone and began texting furiously. "Where's Shay? She was supposed to bring the Polaroid. You know I can't trust mirrors. I am *this* close to panic mode." She held up her thumb and forefinger to show the millimeter between *here* and *panic mode*.

"I think you might be even closer than you think," I said, laughing. I put my arm around her and started sifting through the racks of evening gowns.

Just then, a terrified-looking shopgirl with a blond blunt cut peeked her head around the corner of the rack. "Is there anything else I can get for you, Ms. Benny?"

SBB's head darted up from her phone. "Didn't I tell you to stay behind your curtain? If I have any chance at all of getting in the zone, I *cannot* have strangers devouring me with their hungry eyes while I browse."

"Yes, ma'am," the girl answered meekly, and she disappeared behind a thick leopard print curtain.

SBB looked at me and sighed. "Tell me, Flan. If I have to do all the work of keeping sales associates at a reasonable distance, what am I even paying Shay for? Ugh, where *is* she?"

If SBB's personal stylist Shay had been called in for backup, I knew SBB was taking this event pretty seriously. Even though she had famously complained about Shay's attitude problem in her *New York* magazine profile, everyone knew that their legendary power struggle had often led to some of SBB's most dramatic and often imitated red carpet looks. I also knew that even though SBB would never admit it, it wasn't Shay's blunt, no-BS style that got under SBB's skin—it was that Shay also outfitted Ashleigh Ann Martin on the sly.

"To tell you the truth, I don't know why I even agreed to work with Shay again," SBB ranted. "You should have seen what she sent over to the house this afternoon. I can hardly even call them gowns. Tell me, Flan"—she shook her head incredulously—"do I look like a girl who wants to walk down the red carpet as Gothic Bridal Barbie?"

I stifled a laugh. "I would say no. So did you send the dresses back?"

"Immediately, if not sooner," SBB said, falling into a pink suede chair in the corner. She wagged a finger at me. "I can almost smell Ashleigh Ann Martin behind this. It absolutely reeks of her ill will."

"SBB," I said, trying to steer the conversation away from AAM. "You know any dress in this store will look great on you. And you know JR will think you're gorgeous no matter what you're wearing."

SBB heaved a huge sigh from her little body and said, "If only this were about what JR thought."

Then she was out of the chair and pacing the store again with just one green patent leather platform heel on. I could hear her muttering Ashleigh Ann's name under her breath as she rifled through dresses and shook her head.

As I watched her, I started to think about how strange it was that here she was, shopping for her boyfriend's premiere, and the person whom she was really dressing to impress was a girl—a girl she didn't even like. It made me think about Thoney, and about how the pressure to stack up in girls' eyes felt a whole lot more intense than the pressure to impress a guy.

And it hit me that, even today, when I thought I was getting dressed for Alex, I was mostly stressing over what I thought a Thoney girl was supposed to wear. As soon as I got to Wollman Rink, I knew that Alex didn't care what I wore. He was just happy to be hanging out. So even though I could recognize that what SBB said was totally backward, I did get where she was coming from. And I had to admit that I didn't feel absolutely terrific about it.

SBB's cell phone interrupted both of our thoughts. The ringtone was set to JR's new single, "I'm Taking Hot With Me," and she seized it on the first ring from the top of a stack of bejeweled sweaters.

"Shay?" she practically panted. "Tell me you're en route." In a second, her mouth dropped open. "Oh, hi . . . Gloria," she said, drawing out the name. She turned to meet my eyes. "Didn't I tell you not to call me? Didn't I divorce you just six months ago?"

Gloria was SBB's movie-star mother, who I'd always thought meant well, but who drove SBB to even crazier dimensions than she was capable of on her own. After Gloria had fired SBB from the set of *Turn Signal*, a mother-daughter road trip movie they were starring in together in an attempt to "bond," SBB had filed for divorce and had been struggling with her lawyers over the whole mess for months. I took SBB's hand to show my preemptive support.

"A break in your schedule?" SBB said, kicking the green heel off and clutching a clothing rack for support. "You want to come to Jake's premiere?" Her eyes locked on mine and her voice was stiff. "I don't know if that's a good idea, Gloria. You can't just read an article about me in a magazine and waltz back into my life. I'm trying to pick up the pieces and move on. . . . Yes. . . . Well, things have been very hard for me, too." More pacing. "What do you mean, it's not my decision?" Big sigh. "Then why did you call me in the first place? What? I can't believe—fine! I *will* see you there!" The second SBB clicked off her phone, she let out a howl that sounded like a cross between an enraged elephant and a crying cat. She threw herself down on the zebra print area rug at our feet, closed her eyes, gripped her hands into fists, and let out another giant screech of frustration as she curled into the fetal position. I put my arms around her in a hug.

"We're fine." I motioned to the terrified salesgirl, who'd popped out her head again in fear.

"No, we're not!" SBB wailed.

"You can do this, SBB," I said. "It's just now you have to look doubly extra-specially amazing next week."

Luckily, at that moment, the door chimes jingled again and in walked Shay McCruthers, dressed head to toe in black leather with two Polaroids slung over her shoulder, a wheeled garment bag, and a portable aromatherapy set.

Instantly I felt relieved on SBB's behalf. Shay may have caused SBB some grief in the past, but she definitely knew how to calm her down.

"You're late," SBB fumed, uncurling herself from the carpet.

"Save your breath," Shay said before SBB could go on. "I came prepared, and it's better late than never, and I really don't have the time or the energy right now to hear about it from you. Let's just get down to business."

For a second SBB looked like she didn't know whether to kick Shay or hug her, but finally she just nodded and said, "You're right. We don't have any time to waste."

Soon the two of them were in full dressing mode. Shay snapped pictures of SBB in a floor-length gold lamé get-up, a fitted red crepe cocktail dress, and a shimmery brown tulle gown. I could tell that SBB was already in a much better place, so I sank into the hot pink chair and let out a deep breath.

When SBB emerged from the dressing room in a green retro shift dress, I gasped. "That might be the one," I said.

She bobbed her head. "*One* of the ones," she corrected. "But you're right. I'm feeling the good vibes, too."

She climbed up on a platform while Shay marked places for alteration with a mouthful of straight pins.

"Stand still," she commanded, "or we'll be here all night."

SBB gritted her teeth and stared down at Shay. "I have an idea. How about don't jab your pins of death into my multimillion dollar–insured skin? Then I won't *have* to squirm, will I? Anyway, Flan," she said, sucking in her breath and turning to me, "how much longer do I have to wait to hear about your date with the Prince? If I have to think about Gloria for one more second, I swear I'm going to explode."

I smiled. And blushed. "Oh . . . it was good," I said. "It was really good."

"Boring!" she cried. "I still have images of my mother in my head! Give me details! Give me hot moments! Give me something to work with here! I'm practically pinned down on a platform and all you can offer me is 'good?'"

Shay shook her head. "Do you want to be permanently pinned to this platform?" she asked. "Because you can take your attitude and—"

"And what?" SBB said, hands on her waist. "And go out and hire your nemesis to be my next personal shopper? Don't think I don't know you've been working with Ashleigh Ann on the side."

Shay looked up and pointed a finger at SBB, like she was going to come back and tell her off. But instead of saying anything, she just held out her finger and her death stare until, miraculously, SBB sniffed and looked away.

"That's what I thought," Shay muttered. I'd never seen anything like it.

"Well, it was just a first date," I butted in, trying to break some of the tension. "I think he likes me, but he's a little edgier than the other guys I've been out with, so . . ."

I trailed off when I realized they were still too busy with their power struggle to listen. Maybe SBB and Shay would be better off if I scooted out of the way. And didn't I have something else I needed to do tonight? Oh yeah . . . that little thing called homework. And that's when I realized that it was already nine o'clock and the store would've been closed except that the poor shopgirl was still stuck behind her curtain. I went to check on her and there she was, leaned against the wall with her arms folded, half asleep.

"You can come out now," I said. "It's okay."

The girl smiled at me and immediately darted past SBB, who didn't even notice her.

"Hey, SBB," I said, standing up to gather my things. "I should probably get going. I've got a quiz tomorrow morning. You're going to look incredible in that dress next week."

A look of panic washed over SBB's face.

"But this is only Option One. What about Option Two?" she said. Then, looking down at Shay and dropping her voice to a whisper, she added, "Just in case of . . . you know . . . WS."

I felt the weight of my school books in my bag and

the weight of SBB's puppy dog eyes full of Wardrobe Sabotage worry pulling me in opposite directions. I didn't know what to do.

"Well, what if I come over on Friday and check out what you come up with for Option Two? That will still give you enough time to make adjustments if you need to, right?"

SBB exhaled gratefully. "That sounds great. Good luck on your quiz." Her hand went to her neck where she fiddled with the clasp of a necklace.

"You're still fidgeting!" Shay shouted from below.

"Silence or I'll step on you with these heels!" SBB said. She turned to me: "Flan, I can't believe I almost forgot!"

"Forgot what?" I asked.

She handed me the gold necklace she'd been wearing. "It's for you. Penn DiMontagne gave it to me when we were shooting *Loan Shark of Venice Beach*. I thought it might give you good luck in class."

I opened the locket and read the phrase: *All that glisters is not gold.*

As I leaned forward so SBB could fasten it around my neck, I recalled the scene in *The Merchant of Venice* where the Prince of Morocco reads this line inside the gold casket. Maybe I was finally picking up this stuff.

"This is great, SBB," I said. "Thank you so much."

"Good night, fair Flan," SBB called out as we air-kissed, and I started for the door. "You're more Shakespearean already!"

The good news was, I loved the necklace. The bad news was, I didn't think it was going to do much to help me on my quiz tomorrow morning.

Chapter 14

*G*ood work today, girls. Shower off and meet back here in ten for a huddle," a red-faced, sweaty Ramsey called out the next day after practice. All fifteen of us were back in the school's locker room, although Ramsey looked like the only one who actually needed a shower.

The rest of us were still glad to take the ten-minute break as we changed back into our street clothes. It was Thursday, and just as Camille had promised, it was Theme Day among our group of friends. Last night, Morgan had sent out the email detailing the directive to dress as "punk rock chic," and Camille and I had met in the locker room this morning to compare vintage graphic tees and black leather Derek Lam berets.

Now, as we pulled on our rocker duds for the trip home, Camille groaned. "I'm so done with the huddling," she muttered to me, rubbing some MOR Pomegranate lotion on her hands. "I've been huddling for the past two hours, and I'm tired. The only good thing about huddling on the field is that it gives me three shielded minutes away from Xander seeing how much I completely suck at field hockey."

"Camille," I teased as I slipped out of my cleats and back into my ancient Doc Martens, "remember what we talked about?"

"Yeah, yeah, yeah," she said in a rehearsed voice as she tugged on her fishnets. "You think Xander already likes me enough, so it doesn't matter that the field hockey ball seems to have a magnetic attraction to my face." She sighed. "Don't get me wrong, I'm psyched that he comes to watch practice, but the whole time I'm so focused on him that I'm definitely not getting any better at the game."

Even though I wasn't quite as field hockey challenged as Camille, I knew what she meant. As soon as I saw Alex join the sidelines with the other boys, my heart started racing, and it wasn't from the long sprint I'd just taken toward the goal. But after a few minutes of blushing and heart-thumping, I decided it was cool that he'd shown up—especially when he gave me a hello hip check on the sidelines after practice.

Looking over at Kennedy and Willa, I felt relieved

that Alex had been the only person hip checking me tonight. The two of them were already seated on the bench for Ramsey's post-practice huddle, but in the meantime, it looked like they were gathering in a huddle of their own. Half the team was standing around them, listening to Willa go on and on about the after-party for her father's movie premiere.

"And then Darren Shaw—you know he's in that new cowboy movie—he wanted to take me to Pastis, but I told him, 'I won't set foot in that place after what happened to my father.'"

"What happened to your father?" Faiden asked expectantly, playing right into Willa's hands.

"Well, it was two summers ago and Daddy ordered the lobster bisque, but when they brought it out . . ."

"Somebody put me out of my misery," Camille groaned to me under her breath. "Do you think she ever gets sick of hearing her own voice?"

"What I can't understand is why no one else does," I said, fitting my beret back over my hair.

"Oh my God," Willa said, interrupting her own riveting story and using her thumb and pointer finger to pick up a pair of track pants that were lying on the floor. "Whose *are* these? You could fit, like, four of me in them."

Within seconds, every girl in the locker room had

disowned the pants with some version of "no way" or "those are massive."

What no one was saying, and what we all knew, was that the pants belonged to Ramsey. I gritted my teeth.

Sure, Ramsey was a big-boned girl, but there was nothing outrageous about the size of her pants. The only thing that was outrageous was Willa making such a big deal out of them.

Kennedy busted out laughing, and the two of them jumped up to take turns holding the pants to their own much smaller waists.

"Wanna see if we can both fit inside them?" Kennedy whispered to Willa. "You take the right leg, I'll take the left."

I shot Camille a look. I'm sure she was also remembering the stunts Kennedy had pulled in the locker room back at Miss Mallards. Back then I didn't have whatever it would take to stop her. But as I listened to Ramsey showering not ten feet from where Kennedy and Willa were making a huge joke of her pants, the only thing I could think of was that someone had to stop them before Ramsey saw what they were doing. I mean, Ramsey didn't deserve a cruel practical joke—all she ever wanted was to run a great freshmen field hockey team.

"Give me the pants, Kennedy," I said, holding out my hand.

"Oh, are these yours, Flan?" Kennedy said. "I mean, I knew you'd put on some weight, but not *that* much." The two of them doubled over with laughter. A couple of the girls laughed with them, but the others just looked uncomfortable.

Then I heard the sound of the shower stop and, without a word, I yanked the pants out of her hands. "This is stupid," I said, "and it's mean. Don't play on the team if all you care about is making fun of the captain. You can be bitchy from the sidelines if that's your thing."

Willa sneered. "Don't act like it's not your thing too, Flan. You think you can come in here and play the sweet innocent card this week just to win Virgil Host? I hate to tell you, but you're a whole lot more transparent than you think. Deep down, you're not any different from us."

As I looked at Willa's perfect features all twisted up in a smirk, the first thing that went through my mind was SBB's reference to Willa being a chubby kid—and here she was making fun of Ramsey for being tall and athletically built. How many people here knew what she used to look like? But the second thing that ran through my mind was that if I used that as my trump card now, I *wouldn't* be any different from Willa and Kennedy.

For so long, I'd been wanting to have the perfect comeback to their catty comments, but maybe *not* having that talent was the point. I didn't want to play their games. I didn't want to be anything like them.

I shook my head at Willa, because at that moment, I genuinely felt sorry for her. "Drop the pants," I said. "It's stupid."

"There a problem?" Ramsey's voice echoed throughout the room as she crossed the cement floor with a towel wrapped around her head.

"Not at all," Kennedy said, sickly sweet, taking the pants from Willa's hand and holding them out to Ramsey. Ramsey seemed to notice nothing and just slid them into her bag.

"Good," she said, motioning for us to gather around her. "Now, I need to ask your help with a serious issue we're having on the team."

We sat down on the benches around Ramsey. "Some of you may know that I'm not really one to get all obsessed with 'fashion,' but I've been given a directive that the team needs new uniforms. For some of you, the way you look might affect the way you play, so I want everyone to weigh in on what our move is here."

"Why don't we just pick them out from a catalog and buy them?" a blond pigtailed girl named Jane asked. "It's not like anyone can't afford it."

Ramsey shook her head. "You know the Thoney policy—no individual purchases. We have to raise the money ourselves."

"Well, how much do they cost?" Camille asked. "We could do a bake sale or a car wash or something."

"What is this, nineteen eight-five in Indiana?" I heard Willa mutter to Kennedy. "A *bake sale*? And who among us knows how to wash a car?"

Ramsey nodded, combing through her wet hair. "It's an idea, but the problem is that our first game is coming up in less than two weeks, and we need the uniforms made by then. Can we organize a bake sale by then that would make enough money? You wouldn't believe how expensive . . ." She trailed off.

I wanted to help. Ramsey fretting over clothing sounded almost funny to me because it was so not her territory.

And just like that, I had an idea. I turned to Ramsey, who was looking more and more dejected.

"I'm not sure whether or not it will work, but I have a friend who might be able to help. Can I get back to you tomorrow?"

Ramsey grinned. "Of course!"

The huddle broke up, and I was just starting to work out the details of how to make my plan happen when I felt someone grab my elbow.

"I know you were really into Ramsey's pants," Kennedy said. "But some of us *don't* want to look like clowns on the field."

Willa brushed her silky blond hair over her shoulder and said loudly, "Don't worry about it, Kennedy. A hundred bucks says she's lying about having a fashion contact. This is just one more pathetic attempt to get Virgil votes."

They giggled as they exited the locker room. The door swung shut behind them, followed by the sound of a couple of snickers. But I could barely hear anything over the sound of blood rushing to my head. Being nice might have been the right thing to do, but at that moment, I really wanted to take the evil duo down.

Chapter 15

*A*s soon as I left the locker room, I dialed Feb's number, praying as it rang that she was still on this continent.

"*Allo?*" a distinctively French voice answered.

"Feb?" I said. It was so like my sister to chameleon herself into whatever her pet project du jour was.

"*Non,*" the voice responded. "It's Jade, *chérie.* Is this my model? Is this Flan?"

"Oh . . . *oui,*" I said, already feeling nervous about thinking I could get Jade to agree to my plan. "Where are you guys?"

Jade sighed heavily into the phone. "We are at a *boite,* at Marquee. Your sister is working out a business deal with the owners to host an after-party for our little show. It's very boring, *ma petite,* but what can I say?" And then she sighed her incredible weight-of-the-world sigh.

I imagined Jade lounging out on the golden banquettes at Marquee, yawning as she watched Feb in power-mode ascend the arc-shaped staircase that led to the VIP room so she could work out the details for a blowout after-party.

"Okay," I said. "I was going to head home and study, unless—"

"Darling, you're young," Jade interrupted. "School can wait until another day. Come keep me company, and we'll talk all about your modeling career."

I gulped, but then I thought about the field hockey team. . . .

"I'll hop in a cab and meet you there in twenty," I said.

"Ah, but don't rush! I do not like all this rushing you New Yorkers do. Take your time, yes? We shall be here. . . ."

People complain about having to wait in lines around the corner just to get to the front door of Marquee, but when the taxi dropped me off on Tenth Avenue at seven o'clock on Thursday, there wasn't even a red velvet rope outside the door. A security guard eyed me warily as I pushed through the door.

"I.D. please," he barked.

I wasn't used to having to show my nonexistent

I.D. to anyone. Usually, I was on the guest list or on the arm of my sister or brother. At least I was still dressed uncharacteristically as a punk rocker. . . . Maybe I'd pass for at least eighteen.

Then I heard Jade's voice call out, "Is okay. She's with me."

Immediately, the security guard made himself scarce. I grinned at Jade and joined her in the candlelit lounge.

I'd been to Marquee a couple of times before, once for Patch's eighteenth birthday party and once for some publicity thing SBB was doing for Peter Marcus's hair-care line. Both times, the clientele had been the eye candy—the place was always jam-packed with gel-haired guys in dark suits and Hermès ties and girls with a hundred different couture variations on the same little black dress.

Tonight, the place was practically empty except for Jade Moodswing, all in black again and standing out dramatically against the shimmery gold wallpaper. Jade motioned to a bartender hanging out behind the enormous mahogany track lit bar. In seconds, he whisked over a refill in a martini glass for her and a bottle of Paul & Joe Pellegrino for me.

Jade gave me the closest thing I'd seen to a smile, which was really more of a friendly pout and said,

"How have you been since the night I so brilliantly discovered you?"

"Good," I said, thinking about all the running around I'd been doing since then. "Busy, but good."

Jade took a tiny sip of her martini and said, "I hope the busy schedule is leaving you enough time for modeling. We're going to get started next week, and I'm still waiting for you to say *bien sûr*. The show is Thursday at five thirty."

A few days ago, I'd been *unsure* about saying *bien sûr* to modeling because I wasn't sure I was model material. Now it was also a question of scheduling. Resisting the urge to pull out my day planner (which I'd been doing a lot of these days) in the middle of Marquee, I scanned my brain for conflicts.

Thursday was SBB's big night of potential Wardrobe Sabotage at the premiere, but that was later in the night, and I could *probably* squeeze this in first. My head swam thinking about how busy I'd been this week, just keeping up with life at Thoney, hanging out with Alex, courting votes for Virgil, getting involved in field hockey . . . whoops! I'd gotten so mesmerized again by Jade's chicness that I'd almost forgotten what I was doing here in the first place.

"Jade," I said, "I have a favor to ask of you."

She raised an eyebrow. "And here I thought I was the one asking favors of you."

"It's just—" I tried to think of a cool way to dress up what I wanted to ask Jade to do. I could see Feb's silhouette behind the Frank Lloyd Wright–style glass windows of the VIP room upstairs. Her arms were flailing wildly in the air, and I heard her shout the words, "We're just not going to pay that ridiculous price unless you can *guarantee* that people will *literally* feel transported to the south of France."

I realized I might only have a few more minutes alone with Jade. Feb was the queen of storming out on a conversation if she didn't get her way.

"The thing is," I said, "I just joined the field hockey team at school and we're in desperate need of new uniforms. And the first game is in less than two weeks. And we don't have a way to raise the money and have them ordered and shipped and—"

"And you were wondering if I would help you with your uniforms?" Jade said, crossing her legs.

I nodded sheepishly. It sounded a little preposterous to ask a rising design star for help with athletic wear, but Jade's face brightened as she seemed to think about it.

"*Chérie,* I will tell you a story. Last week, I sat in

on filming of American TV show with Heidi. I believe is called *Project Runway*? Wonderful people, you Americans. Get such a bad reputation." She turned to face me. "What I'm saying is, *chérie*, your little favor reminds me very much of one of these . . . challenges? I like it. Maybe it will help me keep my mind off the Armory show all the time. A little fun. We can sit down next week and look at some samples—"

"Jade, thank you so much!" I said, resisting the urge to tackle her with a giant bear hug.

Jade held up a finger to stop me. "I will love to help you, Flan, on one condition."

"Okay," I grinned, knowing what was coming. "I'll be your model."

Jade beamed, raised her martini to my Pellegrino, and said, "*Parfait!* This is good news. I will design skirts for hockey, you will do catwalk, and you can bring all of your friends to the show. Everything we do together is brilliant! You shall see . . ." But then she sighed and fell back against the bar in complete exhaustion after all that enthusiasm. "Yes," she said, "so American, so brilliant . . ."

Speaking of brilliant, I had to pat myself on the back for this one. A French fashion designer to the rescue for our field hockey uniforms? The girls on the team would be *très* psyched about this one.

*I*f there's one way to get a reality check that you are not, in fact, living the life of a professional model, it's sliding your tray along the lunch line in the Thoney cafeteria. On Friday afternoon, I was in line behind Dara, who was lamenting the fact that she'd just bombed a quiz in biology. When she sighed and nabbed the very last order of fries—the very last edible item in the line—I was left face-to-face with a lone hot turkey sandwich under the heat lamp. What Would Jade Moodswing Do?

For starters, Jade Moodswing probably wouldn't have been so late to lunch because she probably wouldn't have hung around after her English class was dismissed to talk to Mr. Zimmer about act structure. But I was still wigging out about how tough I was finding all this *Merchant of Venice* stuff and was looking for a way in with Mr. Zimmer. This was the sort of thing my siblings would have made endless amounts of fun of me for. But while I knew they would have called it sucking up, I called it getting more accustomed to the Thoney way of courting favors.

Dara popped a fry in her mouth and turned to me at the end of the line. She said, "All I need is for someone to sit down with me, talk to me like I'm a four-year-old, and explain the difference between mitosis and meiosis."

Gingerly placing the turkey disaster on my plate, I said, "I'll help you." The words just kind of popped out—offering up my time seemed to be my first instinct these days.

"Seriously?" she said, holding out the plate of fries for me to share as we walked through the cafeteria together.

"Seriously," I said. "I took bio last semester, and my teacher gave us all these mnemonic devices for keeping track of that stuff. It'd be easy for me to go over it with you."

"You just totally made my day," Dara said, laying down her tray on the table where she sat with Olivia and Veronica.

"What made your day?" Veronica piped in. She was chewing on the eraser of her pencil, furrowing her brow over an open geometry book. "Ooh," she said, looking up at us. "Fries. Way tastier than my eraser."

Dara held out the fries to Veronica. "Flan's going to tutor me in bio. She took it last semester at Stuy and is going to save my life before I fail another quiz."

Veronica closed her math book and sighed. "Any chance you also took geometry last semester? I'm literally drowning in the Pythagorean theorem."

"Actually, I did," I said, suddenly feeling a bit better about my Shakespeare woes. In a weird way, it helped to know that I wasn't the only one who thought the classes here were hard. "I got an A last semester in geometry. It's pretty simple once you get the hang of the formulas."

"Whoa," Veronica said, looking at me like I was suddenly speaking Latin. "I'd give anything to be able to put the words 'simple' and 'geometry' in the same sentence." She put up her hands in a prayer pose. "Could we please, please do a joint tutoring session tonight—bio for Dara and geometry for me? Pleeease, Flan, you would *totally* be our hero."

"You really would." Dara nodded, her red curls bobbing at her shoulders. "We'd owe you big time."

"Of course, you guys," I said, shrugging. "You don't have to owe me anything. I'm happy to help you."

Dara and Veronica were becoming my friends, so it seemed obvious that I'd be there for them to help with study questions, but when I thought about it, this would also probably bring me some good karma—and some secured votes—for Virgil Host.

Sure, Willa could hand out invites to some movie screening, but I was the one putting in quality study time with our grade.

"When should we do it?" I asked the girls.

"ASAP," Dara said. "My next quiz is next week, and I need all the help I can get."

Veronica thumbed through the screen of her iPhone. "How about today, right after school?"

I pulled out my planner too, and I tried to decipher my own handwriting to make sense of all my scribbled plans for the week. "I've got field hockey practice until five o'clock," I said, although on my to-do list for tonight I'd actually written down: "Do homework" (something I probably shouldn't need a reminder to get done). I looked up at Dara and Veronica, who were waiting, iPhones poised, to plug me into their evenings. And once again, I realized that my own homework would have to wait until later. "Why don't I meet you guys at 71 Irving Place for a coffee and study break after practice?"

"Perfect," they both said at once.

When I finally made my way over to the third table, Camille was standing up to clear her tray.

"Hey," she said. "I was wondering where you were. I've been wanting to talk to you."

"Sorry," I said. "I had to stay late to help Mr. Zimmer with something, then I got caught up with Dara and Veronica, and now lunch is basically over and . . ." I trailed off, looking at my watch. "What was it you wanted to talk to me about?"

Camille blushed her classic tell-tale boy problem red.

"Ooh," I teased her. "Do you have a date with someone special?"

"Ugh," Camille groaned, turning even redder against her white cashmere turtleneck. "Not even. That's what I wanted to talk to you about. Either he hates the way I play field hockey or—"

"*Camille*."

"Okay, okay, or both of us are just way too shy around each other. I like him so much—I mean did you see his haircut yesterday at practice, how it's all lopsided and adorable? Anyway, I just feel like nothing's ever going to happen." She crossed her arms on the table and lay her head down so her long hair cascaded over her face. "Why am I so relationship challenged? Why can't Xander be like Alex and just ask me to hang out?"

I lifted the curtain of her hair so I could see her

face. "What if *you* suggest hanging out?" I said, knowing she never would. "Why does it have to be the guy who does it? If you want something," I said, thinking at that moment about Virgil, "why don't you go out and get it?"

"Argh," Camille squealed and hid back under her hair. "Way too scary." She giggled. "You can say that because you're so much more comfortable with Alex than I am with Xander. I mean, I've liked him for*ever*." I could tell she was working on an idea from the way her eyes scrolled back and forth. "Hey," she said finally. "What if you . . . you know . . . what if we all hung out together?"

"A double date?" I said, picturing the four of us whirling around Wollman Rink. "That sounds like the perfect solution."

"Yay!" Camille squeezed my hand. "When can we do it? This weekend?"

Again, I pulled out my planner and flipped through the scribbled-on pages. When I got to the weekend, for a second I couldn't believe how white and wide open the squares for Saturday and Sunday were. Then I remembered that I'd promised to join my mom up at our country house in Connecticut for a decompressing weekend—which I suddenly realized that I desperately needed.

"I'll be at our country house this weekend," I told Camille, flipping through to next week's appointments. "But I'm supposed to meet up with Alex after practice on Monday night. You should stick around, and I'll tell Alex to make sure Xander comes, too."

As I jotted this down, Camille laughed. "You really have an organized system going on there," she teased.

"Hey," I protested as we walked out of the cafeteria arm-in-arm. "Thoney life is hectic. There should be a class where they teach us how to keep up!"

Chapter 17

T didn't realize how badly I needed to recharge until Saturday morning when I came up for some country air. After the two-hour drive to our summer house in Connecticut, my mom and I were lounging around in our bathrobes on the loveseat in the kitchen. We'd picked up our traditional latte and croissant combo from Tartine and had the whole spread laid out on a silver tray.

"You know, darling," my mom said, dipping a tiny edge of a buttery croissant into her coffee, "at first I was disappointed that your father forgot to mention his golf tournament in Maui this weekend. But now that we're here together, I'm so glad to have a girls' weekend with you."

I squeezed her hand and watched an owl roosting in one of the giant pine trees on our property. It felt like it had been a long time since I'd been up here, since I'd seen any bird besides a Central Park pigeon. I'd forgotten how good it felt to get away from the rush of city life and just chill out.

"I'm glad to have a girls' weekend, too." I said.

"I wish February had been able to join us." My mom furrowed her brow, which I knew was against her dermatologist's orders. "I worry about her, all of her undertakings. She's so passionate, but she over-extends herself." Then her face smoothed out, and she turned to look at me. "I'm glad I don't have to worry about the same thing with you, Flan. You've always known how to take it easy. Sometimes I think the rest of us should take a lesson from you."

For a second, I almost took my mom's words seriously—I almost said something like "I think I could squeeze you in for a lesson." It was ridiculous, but I'd been so hung up on saying "yes" to everything anyone asked me to do this week that at this point it felt instinctual.

I started to laugh. "Oh, Mom, I think I might have left that Flan somewhere on the front steps of Thoney. Recently, I've been feeling a lot more like Feb."

"What do you mean?" my mom said. "Are you falling under the spell of that Jade Moodswing, too?"

"Well," I said, "maybe. She is pretty great. In fact, I might have made Ramsey's whole season when I told her that Jade agreed to design our field hockey uniforms. And when I told the girls that they all could come see the fashion show, everyone was ecstatic."

"It's fantastic," my mom said. "Your father and I really can't wait for this fashion show. The idea of our two girls working on it together. . . ." She looked at her watch. "Which reminds me, I've scheduled a little surprise in honor of your first catwalk appearance."

Just then, the doorbell rang, and when I answered it, two blond women in white uniforms walked in without a word. Behind them, two blond men wheeled in contraptions that I soon realized were folding massage beds.

"Right on time!" my mom exclaimed. "How about setting those up here in the living room where we get the soft morning light?" She monitored the progress of our living room's transformation as the Swedish foursome arranged the beds, drew the blinds, and lit aromatherapy candles. "How's this for R&R?" she asked me.

"Redefined," I said, shaking my head at the masseuse's silent diligence. "This is amazing, Mom."

When everything was set up, the two men filed out the front door, and the women motioned us toward the side-by-side beds.

"Here," one of them said brusquely. "You will lie down."

I didn't argue, just arranged myself facedown on the table and let the relaxation begin.

"So," my mom said, her voice slightly muffled by the headrest she was lying on. "How do you rate your first week at Thoney? Are you feeling settled yet?"

"I guess so," I said as the verbally-challenged masseuse began working on a knot in my neck that I didn't even know I had. "But I think my calendar is booked for the rest of the semester."

"You're a Flood—you make friends easily," my mom said, like it was the most natural thing in the world.

"I guess. It's just getting hard to keep track," I said. "Yesterday, I accidentally double-booked myself. I was tutoring some Thoney girls and forgot that I'd told SBB I'd go over some costuming options for Jake Riverdale's movie premiere."

"I'm sure SBB understands," my mom said. "She certainly knows what it's like to keep up with a busy calendar. And she'll be all right at the premiere—she's always had a good eye for fashion."

"I know," I said. "But it was more than that. SBB was also supposed to tutor me on some Shakespeare stuff for my English class. Instead, I was the one doing the tutoring for Dara and Veronica. I wanted to help them, but—"

My mom clucked her tongue. "Flan, you have such

a big heart, but you can't be accountable for everyone else to the point where you forget to be accountable for yourself. I'm glad you're here, so I can be accountable for you just relaxing."

"I know," I said, finally feeling myself sink deep into the massage table. "I'm glad, too."

"If I've told you once, I've told you a thousand times: You're my most responsible child. But I know we're not around much to keep an eye on you, and I want you to promise me that you'll take care of yourself."

"Okay," I said, letting out a slow yawn. "I promise. It's just this Virgil thing. I think that's why I keep saying 'yes' to everything anyone asks me to do. I feel like the nicer I am, the closer I get to having it in the bag."

"I know I've told you about when I was Virgil Host," my mom said, and I prepared myself to hear, for the hundredth time, about the shell-pink Chanel pantsuit she wore when she was Host, about the debate she practiced for a week—back when Virgil was more than just a party—and about the date she'd had flown in from Andover a few months before she'd met my dad.

Then my mom surprised me when she said, "But I haven't told you how I *won* the election."

I popped my head up from the massage table. "No," I said, "you haven't."

Just then I felt a strong pressure on my head and realized the masseuse was practically wrestling my neck back down on the table. "You will relax," she said roughly, like it was an order.

"Yes, ma'am," I said meekly, lowering my head again. "So how'd you win, Mom?"

My mom sighed. "It's not something I'm proud of." She cleared her throat. "There was this girl. Her name was Harriet Dawson. I still remember—she had these press-on fake red nails, sharp as daggers. I guess you could say she was the Kennedy of my high school years. As you can imagine," my mom said, "the competition between us was stiff."

I thought about Willa and the look on her face when she'd told me not to run for Host. "Yeah, I can see that," I said.

"Well, two days before the election, I'd heard a rumor that Harriet might edge me out. I knew she had a big crush on Uncle Owen—you know he used to have that enormous 'fro."

I laughed, thinking of the pictures I'd seen of my mom with her older brother, who looked a lot like Patch might look if he let his hair grow about a foot straight out in every direction.

"Well, fortunately," my mom continued, "Owen had a bad case of laryngitis that week. And I got him to agree to take Harriet out. They went to Sardi's for dinner, and that poor girl was so into him that she overlooked how contagious the laryngitis was when he went to kiss her goodnight. You can probably guess the rest."

"You've got to be kidding," I said.

"I wish I were," my mom said. "Two days later, she'd completely lost her voice and couldn't make her oration. And that, my dear, is how I won Virgil Host."

Then both of us busted out laughing, so hard that our masseuses didn't know what to do with us. They tried to chide us with forceful shushes, and my mom's masseuse even whopped her on the head with a towel. But when none of that worked, they just threw up their hands and let us crack up until we could pull ourselves together.

"How could I have lived for fourteen years and not have known that story?" I asked my mom when we finally calmed down.

She looked at me seriously and said, "I don't know." She shook her head. "Maybe I had to wait to tell you until I knew you wouldn't get any ideas. But listening to you today, darling, and hearing how nice—how utterly opposite—your campaign to win has been, I know that I have nothing to worry about.

Besides," she said, winking at me, "Patch is in Caracas this week."

"And I don't think he has laryngitis," I said, laughing.

By then, our masseuses had literally thrown in their towels and given up on creating any sense of serenity in the room. But to me, it didn't matter. I felt more relaxed than I had all week.

$\mathcal{V}$ote for Willa. Vote for Willa. Vote for—" Kennedy
froze in her orange Hollywould flats when she turned
to face Camille and me outside the assembly hall on
Monday morning. It was just before the first bell rang,
and Team Flan had agreed to meet early so we could
make one last-minute push before everyone cast their
ballots for Virgil Host at lunch.

Apparently, Kennedy and Willa had the same idea.
From where I was standing, I could see only the bottom of Willa's snakeskin boots-of-death on the stairwell, but I could hear her voice talking to a group of
girls gathered around her.

"I'm just looking out for the well-being of our
class," she said, making no attempt to lower her
voice. "Do you think Flan Flood even knows what it
means to host a Thoney event? A month ago, she
was a public school nobody!" I could hear the

laughter surround her. Then she said, "I mean, I'm just *saying*."

Now, Kennedy stood before me, with an armful of tiny bouquets of calla lilies tied with a ribbon and fastened with a business card that Willa had produced for the election. Kennedy returned the flower she had begun to hold out to me back to the bunch.

"On second thought," she said, making a big display of pursing her lips together. "Better not waste these." She smiled innocently. "Vote for Willa," she said, her voice dripping with her trademark fakeness, before disappearing around the corner.

"Ugh." I rolled my eyes at Camille. "It's a good thing I had this weekend to unwind. Otherwise, that might have just made me snap."

"I mean, seriously," Camille said, shaking her head. "Who makes a *business card* for this type of thing? I was this close to grabbing that lame bouquet out of her hands and tearing it apart, petal by petal."

I nodded, pantomiming the scene of ripping up the flowers. "Vote for Willa. Vote for Willa. *Not*."

Just then, Harper, Amory, and Morgan waved from across the foyer. As they got closer, I could see that each of them was carrying a differently shaped cardboard box. All three wore buttons in Thoney colors—

gold background and forest green letters—with different fonts reading GET FLOODED.

"Omigod," Camille said, grabbing two more buttons from the box Harper was holding and handing me one. "Amazing. I love all the different fonts. What's in the other boxes?"

Amory opened her box to show stacks of tiny breath mint tins with FLAN FLOOD: A FRESH START spelled out across the top.

"So fun, you guys," I said, truly touched that my new friends were taking this election so seriously.

"And so much more functional than the Willa lilies going around," Morgan said. "Check out my contribution." She opened her own box to reveal a box of burned CDs. The album art was a picture of me scoring a goal on the hockey field, and the title read, FLAN'S GOT YOU COVERED. "It's all cover songs by cool female artists," she explained, handing each of us one.

"Way to go, Morgan. These totally rock." Camille turned to me. "Okay, Flan, show us the real pièce de résistance."

I felt for the invitations to the fashion show that I'd slipped in my messenger bag this morning. Jade Moodswing had brought them over last night in an engraved pewter box, and there were enough gold calligraphed invitations for every girl in our class—even Kennedy and Willa. I opened the box to show my friends.

"Whoa, Pandora," Amory said. "I think you have the Virgil vote in the bag."

"Can I just say how refreshing it is that not only are you part of this totally swanky event, but you're inviting *everyone* to come to it?" Harper said, turning to hand out a few buttons to some girls walking past us. "That *never* happens at Thoney. There's always someone being intentionally left out."

I shrugged. "What's the point of leaving anyone out? Everyone's invited to Virgil, so why shouldn't the host be the kind of person who actually *wants* to hang out with the whole grade?"

"Hey, Flan," I heard a voice call from behind me. It was Shira Riley and a few of her senior friends, including Anna, whose Comptoir bag I had complimented last week. "Anna and I just wanted to swing by and wish you luck today. We heard you've got some vicious competition."

I couldn't believe that these senior girls would even keep up with the relatively small happenings of the underclassmen. Then I wondered: "Did Patch tell you I was running?" I asked Shira.

"Actually," Anna said, giving me a wink that looked

familiar. "My little brother told me all about it after you two hung out at Wollman the other day."

"*You're* Alex's older sister?" I asked, feeling so totally dumb that I hadn't put the pieces together before. He'd definitely mentioned her a couple of times in relation to Thoney and Virgil.

"He's *my* little brother." She corrected the emphasis jokingly. "And he seems to think you'd make a pretty good Host."

Shira nodded. "So do we. We'll do what we can to spread the word. See you around," she said, and the two of them headed down the senior locker hall.

"Way to pick the right boy du jour, Flan," Camille said. Then she pointed to a sign on the door next to the assembly hall. "Hey, check it out. They posted the details about how voting works today."

Morgan learned forward and read aloud from the sheet of tacked-up paper. "Morning assembly has been rescheduled for three o'clock this afternoon. Cast your ballots for Virgil Host in front of the cafeteria during lunch. After an announcement from Headmistress Winters, this month's Host will be revealed."

"I wonder what the announcement from Winters is all about," Camille said. "She usually only makes one appearance at the beginning of the semester to scare the crap out of everyone."

Harper shrugged. "I dunno. Maybe it has something to do with Virgil?"

"Or the spring fund-raiser," Amory said, hoisting her Coach tote higher on her shoulder. "Sometimes she comes out of seclusion to give us some money-grubbing sound bites to send home to our parents."

"Or maybe," Morgan chimed in, "she anticipates wanting to congratulate Flan and her loyal supporters for running the first anti-smear campaign in Thoney history?"

"Speaking of which," Camille said, taking half of the fashion show invitations from my hands. She looked at her watch. "We've got three hours until lunch, girls. Let's go out and spread the word just so we make absolutely sure Flan is the one we're congratulating in assembly this afternoon."

At three o'clock, as requested, the freshman class filed into the ornate, high-ceilinged assembly hall. All day, I'd been jittery, waiting for this moment with a combination of anticipation and nervousness. At lunch, I had to sit with my back to the voting table so I wouldn't see the other girls' faces as they went up to cast their ballots.

My friends had been great about it. Amory, Harper, and Morgan spent their lunch periods passing out our propaganda until the very last minute, while Camille sat with me, trying to distract me with a very original theatrical performance starring animal crackers purchased from the vending machine.

My hands down favorite was: "Here's Willa, the lion on her way to the River Styx for a drink—whoops—she just got her head bit off. Mmm, tasty."

Now, I filed into the third row of the assembly hall,

flanked by my friends and trying not to make eye contact with the real-life version of Willa Rubenstein, whose head was still intact and even more haughtily set than usual.

I looked around the room that just last week had seemed to be filled with girls I didn't know and was slightly intimidated by. But today, almost everywhere my gaze fell, I recognized a girl I'd taken the time to get to know. There was Mattie Hendricks, nose deep in her folder of Student Senate supplies. There was the Dara, Veronica, and Olivia trio, giving me the thumbs up from their row. There was Faiden, flipping her hair in the front. There were the Nail Filers from my English class to whom I'd lent my Burt's Bees cuticle cream on Friday. There was Ramsey, looking up at the ceiling with that concentrated look on her face that I could tell meant she was working out field hockey strategies in her head.

It was definitely a big change from last week, and it made me think about how much fun I'd had getting to know everyone. Even though I'd been making a lot of these efforts so that I could count on people for votes today, I knew that there was more to it than that. If I didn't win Virgil Host today, all the insanity of last week would still have been worth it, because I'd made some real connections with these girls.

Then again, it *would* be really nice to win. . . .

"Attention, attention," Headmistress Winters called out from her podium. I realized I'd been so consumed by my own thoughts that I hadn't even heard the auditorium hush up when the headmistress walked in.

She looked just as regal as she had last week, in a blue St. Johns suit and Donna Karan glasses.

"Good morning, girls," she said slowly. "I know you're all eager for me to make the announcement about which of you will be hosting the first Virgil of the new year." Her gaze swept the room. "But first, I'm sorry to inform you that we have some unpleasant business to attend to."

My friends and I shot each other a confused look.

"As you know," she continued, "Thoney has a large treasury. We take our funds and our fund-raising very seriously. There are strict rules for each organization about how money is to be raised, and there is strict monitoring of how it is allotted." She cleared her throat. "I won't pontificate any longer. Someone has taken a sum of three thousand dollars from the treasury."

A gasp rippled through the room.

"The money was accounted for on Friday. And now it is gone," Headmistress Winters said. "Rest assured, we are looking into this matter very thoroughly. But if anyone knows anything about this unfortunate situation, you are best advised to come forward immediately with the information."

There was a long pause during which I felt the critical eyes of the board of faculty members boring into each and every one of us. They were some powerful gazes. I didn't know a single thing about the missing money, but I still felt incredibly guilty all of a sudden.

"Well," the headmistress said after a painful moment, "I imagine no one is going to come forward in this public forum, so we'll leave the option open for you to come to us." She nodded, as if to change gears, and said, "And now, on to something much more pleasant."

This was it. My brain was still thinking about the loss of the money, but my heart started thudding in my chest.

"It gives me great pleasure to inform you that your first Virgil of the year will be hosted by an exceptional leader in your grade." Yikes. Willa was class president—as in *official*, elected leader. Was that what the headmistress was referring to? In that instant, I resigned myself to the fact that it would make more sense for Willa to have won. All week I'd seen just how much of a fixture she was at Thoney. And I was just—

"Flannery Flood," Headmistress Winters said with

a smile. "Please give her your warmest Thoney round of applause."

It took a minute, and a rib cage nudge from Camille, for it to sink in that I had actually won. Oh. My. God. I did it? I did it!

Shakily I got to my feet and gave a small wave as the auditorium erupted into applause. A couple of girls whistled and so many people were cheering that the headmistress had to thump on the microphone to get our attention again.

"I'm glad you are all so enthusiastic about Miss Flood," she said. "I'm sure it will be a lovely event. And before you are dismissed, without putting a damper on my own congratulations to our new host, I must implore you all once more to please come forward with any information about this egregious theft. You are dismissed."

The din in the auditorium grew louder, and a huge grin spread across my face. Even Headmistress Winters's downer parting words didn't do a thing to kill my buzz. In fact, if I hadn't been surrounded by a hundred other girls, I might have started jumping up and down.

I scanned the room to see if I could catch a glimpse of Willa or Kennedy, but before I could spot them, I was surrounded by people coming up to me with hugs and congratulations.

Mattie tapped me on the shoulder. "I knew you'd win this, Flan," she said. "You're the best thing to happen to Thoney all year. Now, on behalf of the Student Senate, here's the folder with all the historical information about Virgil and all the practical information that might help you plan. The only thing you have to do by Wednesday is confirm with whichever caterer you choose. Let me know if you have any questions."

"Thanks, Mattie," I said, so excited that I gave The Barker a big hug. As I slipped the folder she'd just given me into my bag, vowing to go over it later that night, I felt my phone buzz with a text. It was from Jade Moodswing.

ARMORY FITTING. NOW AS IN NOW. NEED OUR NUMBER ONE MODEL TOUT DE SUITE.

Camille grabbed my elbow.

"Hey, winner," she said, grinning. "Knew you could do it. How does it feel?"

"Awesome," I said. "Overwhelming. Hey, can you do me a favor? I just got an urgent text from Jade and I have to go to The Armory Show for a fitting right now. Would you explain to Ramsey why I'm missing practice?"

Camille's face fell.

"It's for the good of the team," I tried to explain. "I promised I'd help with these uniforms."

Camille rolled her eyes. "Like I care about missing practice?" she said, laughing. "But what about the thing with Xander and Alex? We're supposed to . . . you know . . ."

"Oh, shoot," I said, slapping my forehead. Since when was I so flaky about plans with my best friend? "The double date. I'm so sorry, Camille. Can we reschedule? How about Wednesday?" I was looking at her but my feet were already moving me away. I said, "I'll call Alex and take care of it. It's my fault, I'll fix it."

"Okay, but you promise we'll do it on Wednesday?" Her eyes looked serious.

"Promise!" And with that, I gave Camille a quick hug and ran to hail a cab.

Chapter 20

$\mathcal{T}$wenty-sixth and Lexington, please," I called to the cab driver who swerved to a mad stop outside Thoney in response to my frantic flagging. The last time I'd darted across town to talk fashion with Jade Moodswing, I'd been in a very different mental place—nervous about whether I could sway Jade to help with our field hockey uniforms, recovering from my face-off with Willa and Kennedy in the locker room, and pretty much consumed by whether or not I could swing this whole Virgil thing my way.

In just a few days, all of those issues had miraculously worked out for the best. Jade was going to be a total lifeline with the uniforms, and I'd won the ultimate battle against Willa. I still couldn't believe I was going to be Virgil Host. I leaned back in my seat as the taxi whizzed downtown and wondered: If all these things were falling into place, why did I still feel so frazzled?

As the taxi passed the Empire State Building, I pulled out my phone to text Alex.

VIRGIL WIN, I wrote. STILL CAN'T BELIEVE IT. LAST MINUTE COMMITMENT TO FIELD HOCKEY UNIFORM DESIGNER JUST CAME UP. WOULD YOU HATE ME IF I ASKED TO RESCHEDULE FOR WEDNESDAY?

Just before the cab stopped in front of The Armory Show, I got Alex's response.

CONGRATULATIONS! HAD A FEELING YOU MIGHT WIN, AND I'LL BET YOU DIDN'T EVEN BREAK ANY RULES. NO WORRIES—WE'LL CELEBRATE ON WED.

The cab pulled to a stop in front of The Armory Show, which I'd forgotten looked terribly formal from the outside. It was hard to believe that this place could function as a military base from nine to five and then switch gears to become a totally prime spot for a fashion show. As I hauled all my field hockey and school stuff out of the cab, I realized that I had something in common with the Armory. Both of us were moonlighting—and I was ready to shed my student status and get made-over. I followed the poster board arrows up the double staircase in the entryway and soon I found myself inside an enormous drill hall.

Dozens of industry professionals scurried around, covering the giant, Gothic windows with gauzy drapes; laying white tape marks down on the floor; and taking fittings of models.

At the center of it all, I saw Jade Moodswing, sporting a soft green leather beanie, black pants, and a black turtleneck, and looking as calm as if she were hemming a pair of high-waisted jeans. She looked up, saw me, and blew a kiss in my direction.

"*Bonsoir, chérie,*" she called out, waving me over. "You're late, but I forgive you."

"Hi, Jade," I said, looking around to find a spot to drop all my bulky bags. There was so much activity in this room, and I definitely didn't want to be responsible for some model getting taken out by tripping over a field hockey stick.

"Flan, don't put that there. Are you crazy?" I heard my sister yell as she removed my field hockey stick from my hands. "Give me that." She turned to Jade. "Did you tell her that she's late? Did you tell her that we need people who can take fashion seriously?"

"I'm sorry, I'm sorry," I said. "I rushed out of school as soon as I got your text. It's just, today was the Virgil election and—"

Feb's face lit up and she grabbed my wrist. "Did you win?"

I nodded shyly, feeling a few other eyes watching as Feb pounced on me with her congratulations. "Forgiven," my sister said. "Wait till Mom finds out. She'll flip! Now get back there and help Jade go over the designs for your uniforms."

A team of assistants pulled me to the back corner of the room, and Jade started to explain her concept for the show.

"You know, Flan, when you asked me to work with sports team uniform, I said to myself, 'Jade, you don't know sports. What is this *uniform*? Maybe is mistake to pull focus away from runway.'" I felt my throat constrict and prepared myself to hear Jade's apology for having to back out. But she turned to me and nodded. "Then, last night," she said, "I had a dream. A vision. What if uniform *is* catwalk? What if *Project Runway* is more than project? Experiment is reality. Do you see?"

"Um," I stalled. "I thought you were doing an evening wear show?"

"Yes, I am. But I found myself, how do you say . . . inspired by you, Flan. Your freshness. *Très à la mode,* this girl-next-door element. *Et voilà,*" Jade said as she pulled back a screen.

My jaw dropped as I took in the models before me. The first one was wearing a gold lamé polo-style shirt and what I guessed was supposed to be a variation on the field hockey skirt. I stepped forward to examine it more closely. It was nearly floor length and filled out underneath with layers and layers of gold taffeta. Yikes. Was this haute athletic wear or a plantation-era ball gown?

The Scarlett O'Hara model was flanked on one side by another model wearing a skin-tight leather miniskirt version of the uniform with a three-inch tartan print choker. On the other side stood another model whose skirt was *almost* a manageable length, but was held up by glittering suspenders with only a small green bandeau underneath.

"Um, wow, Jade."

"It's *magnifique, n'est-ce pas?*"

Oh, God. What had I done? Sure, the stitch work on all three of the uniforms was *magnifique*, and the gold-on-green pattern was regal, but I wasn't exactly sure how functional any of these was going to be. I didn't see how the models could walk down the catwalk without tripping, much less how any of us could try to wear this in a game. I couldn't help but imagine how disappointed Ramsey would look if she were here right now, and I think it must have shown on my face.

"*Zut alors*," Jade said. "Is it the fleur-de-lis on the back? Too much?"

"No, no," I said, wondering how to phrase this to someone like Jade, who might never have seen a game of field hockey in her life. "It's just . . . the length. And some of the cuts. And those suspenders. Everything *looks* amazing, but I'm worried about how well we'd actually play in them."

Jade frowned and seemed to think this through. "But the long skirts, the suspenders, they are my trademark. Every journalist will be expecting them. Nigel made me swear that I would give him the first photograph."

I looked around at all the models in varying stages of dress—some with the full skirts billowing out, some with straight pins holding the hem at the knees for measurement, and I got an idea.

"What if the line shows an evolution?" I said. "Maybe the show starts out with the more elegant, evening wear–like floor-length gown . . ."

"And the girls walk out with shorter and shorter skirts, more better for playing your sport?" Jade finished my thought.

"Exactly," I said, nodding at Jade. "So that the last model is sporting the true uniform."

"The essence," Jade whispered.

I bit my lip so I wouldn't laugh. She was so brooding and serious,but also so brilliant. "The essence of field hockey." I agreed.

"I like zis girl," one of the models said in a heavy French accent.

"That's good, *chérie*," Jade told her. "Because Flan will be modeling with you on Thursday night." She turned to me. "Flan, I think you should model the final piece. The essence. What do you say?"

"Um . . . I say *oui*," I said, remembering my fall the week before at David Burke's and thinking that it would probably be much safer for me *not* to sport the floor-length piece in heels on a catwalk.

"*Parfait*," Jade said with a resolute nod. "Now all you have to do is learn your line."

"My line?" I asked. I didn't know the fashion show came with a script. I thought about the English quiz I had on Wednesday and just hoped that my line wasn't in Shakespearean English.

As Jade moved away to check something in her Moleskine notebook, one of the models turned to me and rolled her eyes.

"Moodswing is a bit touched in zee head," the model said. "She's giving each of us one word to speak at the end of our walk. She wants zee show to tell some kind of story. It came to her in zee same dream as zee one with zee field hockey uniforms."

"And you think it's a bad idea?" I asked the girl, careful about my tone of voice. Suddenly I felt a little guilty that the same dream that brought Jade the idea to incorporate our uniforms in her show had also led to this.

The model clucked her tongue. "Some of zee other girls are threatening to walk out," she muttered under her breath. "No one has ever asked us to *speak* before. We walk—we do not *talk*. It's very nearly catwalk heresy."

Another model with a black bob and a surly but beautiful face chimed in behind us. "*Oui*. My word is morphology," she said, although with her French accent, it sounded like *morp-oh-lo-gie*. "I will look like crazy person if I have to say that on the runway."

"Silence," Jade said, holding up a finger at us. "I found the word for you, *chérie*," she said to me. "I don't know why I didn't think of this immediately. You will be: *essence*. What do you think?"

I looked at the models to my left and shrugged sympathetically. "Essence" was certainly better than "morphology."

"Essence," I repeated, nodding at Jade. "I think I can handle that."

As Jade dismissed us for the night, I tried not to take the surly model too seriously when she raised her eyebrows at me and said, "Well, you may be zee only one who can."

Chapter 21

*E*ssence?" SBB giggled from inside her closet the next day. "She seriously wants you to belt out the word 'essence' at the end of the catwalk on Thursday?"

"I think so," I shrugged, kicking off my shoes and climbing onto SBB's bed.

My double-date with Alex, Camille, and Xander was tomorrow, the fashion show was in two days, Virgil was in three, and I was spending my last night "off" prepping SBB for her big night.

"Doesn't she know models are meant to be seen and not heard?" SBB asked.

I nodded. "Unfortunately, the models seem to agree with you."

SBB emerged from her closet with her jaw dropped open. "Are we talking model mutiny here?" she squeaked. "The only show I ever did with Valentino had a similar episode. It was then and there that I decided never to listen to anyone who called me a diva." She wagged her finger at me as if I were arguing with her. "There is nothing worse than a model on a tirade. They can go from zero to 'I quit' in less time than it takes to say the word 'essence.'"

"Well, hopefully it doesn't get to that point," I called out to SBB, who had disappeared back into her closet. "There seems to be drama everywhere these days. Apparently someone stole three thousand dollars out of the Thoney trust—and it sounds like it's definitely one of the students."

"Huh," SBB called from the closet. "You wouldn't think anyone at Thoney would *need* to steal."

"I know, right?"

"Now, what am I looking for in here?" she said.

"Plan B," I reminded her. "And then Plan C."

I'd seen the amazing green dress SBB had picked out last week at Nanette Lepore for JR's premiere on Thursday, but since she was the eternal over-preparer, she ended up buying not one, but two more options—just in case Ashleigh Ann Martin tried to pull a fast one on her on the red carpet.

There were some shuffling sounds from the closet, and then SBB slunk out in a fitted pink strapless gown very reminiscent of Cameron Diaz at the Oscars.

"Are you trying to be one of JR's Angels in that?" I joked.

"Very punny, Flan," she said, spinning around in front of her three-way mirror. "Is this Ashleigh Ann envy-worthy enough?"

"Absolutely. Either one would be perfect," I said. I tried to imagine the scene on Thursday night—me, hiding out in the limo, with spare couture in both of my hands. It was hard to believe that by the time SBB would be smiling for the paparazzi, I would have just finished my own modeling jaunt downtown. I stifled a yawn at the thought of all this running around. I was definitely going to go into hibernation this weekend. In fact, I wondered whether I could squeeze in a quick nap before we started in on the Shakespeare SBB had promised to go over with me tonight. . . .

"Flan," SBB snapped in my face, bringing me back to reality. "I said, can you please remind me where you're going to be stationed on Thursday?"

I tried to jog my memory. I had so many places to remember to be this week.

"Um, where you told me to be stationed—across the street from the Paris Theatre, right, in front of F.A.O. Schwarz?" Then, I started to rehearse the lines I'd been fed to keep SBB as levelheaded as possible. "I've got the portable steam presser and your aromatherapy relaxing oils in case you have to do a hectic costume change."

SBB closed her eyes and looked slightly calmer.

"I'll be Bassanio to your Antonio," I said, trying another tack.

"Whoa!" SBB exclaimed, springing up. "Did you just say what I think you just said?"

I laughed and nodded. "I'm as shocked as you are," I said. "I think I just made my first successful allusion to *The Merchant of Venice*. I can't believe this stuff is actually starting to make sense to me." I fingered the locket SBB had given me with the *All that glisters* quote engraved on it. "Probably has something to do with this good luck charm."

SBB stuck a bare shoulder out of the closet. "No," she said. "It has much more to do with the fact that you underestimate how smart you are. I knew you'd pick up Shakespeare quickly. It's just like reading sub-titles. After a while—"

"Stop right there—" I said.

"I'm just trying to explain—"

"No," I said to my friend, who had emerged from her closet a third time in the most beautiful slate-colored tulle and organdy puff dress I'd ever seen. "I mean, stop and spin around so I can see how incredible that dress is. You look like you just hopped out of a fairy tale."

"This one?" SBB scrunched up her face. "You really like it? Omigod, Shay literally dragged me to Zac Posen the other day after you left. She forced me to buy it. Threats were made." SBB played Oscar-worthy victim so well. "Eventually, I was just so sick of arguing with her that I took it. But I'm not really sure it's so me."

She looked down and fingered the mass of soft fabric billowing out around her.

"It's so beautiful," I breathed.

"Well, Gloria has always liked the way I look in slate," SBB mused. Then, again, she wagged the finger at me. "*Not* that I'm bending over backward to impress *her*, just so we're quite clear."

I put my hands up in surrender. "We're clear. I'm just saying I love the dress."

SBB looked in the mirror, and then back at me, and then in the mirror again.

"Level with me, Flan," SBB said, sitting down next to me on the bed. "I've got these two other dresses for Thursday, right?"

"Right." I nodded.

"And say AAM does show up in the same one as me, and I have to run and change." She inhaled deeply and let it out, as if predicting the worst. "Well, it's not like once I change, AAM's going to have the same exact Plan B and race to her limo, too. I mean, our war has been waging for a long time, but I really don't think she's vindictive enough to go there, do you?"

I shook my head. "You're probably right."

"Two dresses are enough, then. And anyway, if Gloria does come through and grace us all with her presence, there's a small chance I might be feeling daughterly, and so I'd want to hang with her and Jake together and not be spending all my time steaming gowns and aromatherapying in the limo with you." She looked up at me. "No offense. That sounds fun for another night, maybe —"

"None taken, SBB." I laughed, waiting to see where she was going with this. "You should definitely spend time with Gloria and JR together."

"We'll see about that. But my point is, Flannie, in a roundabout way . . . I've got this beautiful dress from Zac that you seem to like a whole lot. And you've got this very posh event on Friday night in which you must hold up your status as Virgil Host while simultaneously monopolizing the eyes of the Prince of New York."

"Are you saying what I think you're saying?" I said, feeling a grin spread across my face.

"I'm saying that you're the one who needs to look like you just hopped out of a fairy tale." SBB leaned over me so I could help her unzip the dress. Then she slipped out of it and stood there in her Betsey Johnson lingerie. She handed me the dress. "Take my Plan C to Virgil as a thank you for all your help with my mania this week. I won't take no for an answer!"

Holding the dress in front of me as I stood before the mirror, it was almost like magic: the field hockey clothes I was wearing seemed to disappear, and I did feel the whole fairy tale vibe coursing through me.

"You're my fairy godmother, SBB," I said. "I don't know what to say."

"And you're mine, Princess Flannie," she said, putting her arms around me. "So just say yes!"

Chapter 22

What do you think of this color?" Camille asked me Wednesday in the bathroom right after last period. She was looking in the mirror at her top lip, which was a glossy pomegranate shade, unlike her bottom lip, which was matte berry. In keeping with this unexplained new makeup theme, her left eyelid was charcoal and smoky, while her right lid was gold and shimmery, with an eggplant smudge of Urban Decay crayon lining the lashes.

"Um, I think it's a good thing that I already know you and love you," I teased, tugging her long braid. "Otherwise I might mistake you for Cruella De Vil. What makeup memo did I miss? Did we change theme day to Wednesday this week?"

She tugged my ponytail back. "Flan, it's called *options*! How else am I supposed to know whether I should dress the girl-next-door part or do the glamorous arm candy thing for my date with Xander?"

"Simultaneously," Morgan laughed. "Maybe you should go just like this—that way Xander will get an idea of your range. Like you're capable of being *every* possible type of girl out there."

My stomach twisted up in a knot. Camille did look hilarious, but under all that crazy makeup was a girl whose heart was about to be broken when I gave her the news that I'd been putting off telling her about since I got Jade's voicemail this afternoon.

Jade had scheduled a final, essential ("And you are the essence of essential, *chérie*") rehearsal for this evening, which I was not allowed to miss. I was going to have to postpone our double date—again.

Camille noticed my face and hers fell. "I thought you liked this liner when I bought it last week."

"I do—I love the eggplant," I said, biting my lip. "It's not the liner, Camille, and for the eightieth time, Xander's been in love with you for like five years. I think he already approves of what you look like, no matter what color your lips are. But I have some bad news."

Her half-purple, half-pink lips tightened.

"You're bailing on me *again*?"

"Hey," I said, getting slightly defensive. "It only

happened one other time. You make it sound like I'm a career flake. It's just that this week is so crazy. You should just be happy that I haven't scared you with Jade's threatening voicemail on speaker."

Camille shook her head, and I started to realize that this wasn't just something I could keep apologizing my way out of. I was going to have to prove it. She had liked Xander for such a long time—this was a huge deal for her.

"Camille, I promise, this insanity will all be over soon. Things will go right back to the way they're supposed to be."

"Yeah, well," Camille said, slinging her graphic Anthropologie tote over her shoulder. "You let me know when that happens, and I'll see if I'm free to hang out." She didn't say it meanly, just kind of sadly, and then she walked out of the bathroom.

Morgan started to follow Camille, but just before she got to the door, she turned around and took off her headphones. "We were all so psyched when you won Virgil Host, Flan. Don't be a one-hit wonder, okay?"

I felt terrible. I wanted to collapse in one of the stalls so I could pull myself together. But just when I thought I was alone, I heard a toilet flush, and Ramsey walked out of one of the stalls.

"That didn't sound too great," she said.

"Oh, God," I said, clapping my hand to my forehead. "Ramsey, am I the worst person in the school? I feel terrible. It's just—"

Ramsey stood with her hands on her hips and her feet spread apart—the stance she used just before she gave us a major rallying speech on the field.

"Don't be dramatic," she said. "It's not like you stole the treasury money or anything. You overscheduled. Just make sure you consider your batting average. You're still a rookie at Thoney, you know? We've only had one week with you—and we like you a whole lot—but one or two strikeouts without a solid hitting record, well, it can really drag down your stats."

I nodded. "Thanks, Ramsey. You're right."

"Of course I'm right. Now go do your fashion thing so we can get you back on the team ASAP. We need your offense for the game against Spence." She started walking toward the door and called back at me, "Hope you've been practicing that hip check."

I laughed to myself and thought about Alex. Luckily, hip check practice was one area where I hadn't been slacking. I'd sent Alex a text about tonight just after I'd heard from Jade. I checked my phone but hadn't heard back from him yet. Hmm. I'd have to give him a call later tonight after rehearsal. I definitely didn't want to risk lowering my stats with him.

Twenty minutes later, I was just barely on time to Jade's rehearsal—and still completely consumed with guilt. I hadn't heard from Alex, which made me worry that he totally hated me. But because I was almost late, I was also worried about Jade hating me. So I panted up the stairs and barged into the drill hall, where a row of thirty brooding French models looked up from their stylists' chairs at me.

"Fashionably late is not fashionable in the world of actual fashion, sis," I heard Feb call out to me through her headset. "Come on, let's get you changed."

I sighed and thought about spouting off one of my many legitimate excuses—for instance, does anyone here remember that I'm also a high school student?—but I was getting sort of sick of the "Flan's so busy" pity party, and I decided to just embrace the "Flan's a model" party while it lasted.

I was glad to see some of the models practicing their words as Feb led me to the back of the room.

"Morp-ohhh-loh-gie," yesterday's cranky brunette

mouthed into a mirror, showing some real improvement.

Feb shot me a sideways smile. "What's your word, again?" she asked in a joking tone that let me know that the whole bossy sister act was just for show.

"*Essence*," I said dramatically, raising my eyebrows.

Feb laughed. "Awesome."

I shimmied out of my jeans, and Feb helped me into the newly tailored designer field hockey uniform.

"*Très française, non?*" I said in my best Jade voice as Feb led me to a full-length mirror to see the final product.

I'm not sure what my first full thought was when I got a glimpse of myself in the uniform. It was a combination of "This finally feels totally functional" and "I cannot believe I'm going to walk down an actual catwalk" and "Well, I do look kind of great"—but it was definitely a thrill.

From a distance, the green and gold outfit did resemble a regular field hockey uniform. But up close, the stitch work was intricate, contrasting nicely with the subtle, elegant fleur-de-lis pattern on the fabric. And I had never put on something that fit me more perfectly. The bodice of the top was snug but not constricting, and the skirt was cut just above the knee and had enough swing to it that I knew we'd be able to both tear up the field and twirl around the runway.

"Models! Places! *S'il vous plaît! Vite! Vite!*" came Jade's voice through a microphoned headset.

Feb tousled my hair. "*Très* chic! Now get out there and become the essence of runway."

I scurried up the stairs to join the other models on the stage. On our side of the curtain, it was dimly lit and cluttered with technical equipment, but there was a buzz of nervous energy lighting up the air. When a black-clad five-piece jazz band began playing music down below us, everything started to happen so fast. One by one, the girls in front of me started strutting their stuff. I watched their hips jut perfectly from side to side, unendingly impressed that they made walking in crazy platforms look like a barefoot jog on the beach. I just hoped I could keep up.

When it was my turn, I got a nudge from one of the models who'd already gone and started walking. It was hard to see anything past the runway because of all the lights, and I tried not to think about how many people would fill up this room tomorrow. Somehow, through my nerves, I put one gold tighted foot in front of the other and made it to the end of the catwalk. I paused to give Jade what she wanted.

"Essence," I called out, with as much all-American attitude as I could muster. When I turned on my high heel—gracefully—and walked back up the runway, I definitely felt the rush.

Backstage, I heard my cell phone ringing and kicked off my shoes so I could make it over to my bag in time. I caught it just before it went to voicemail and was glad I did. It was Alex.

"Hey!" I said, my heart still beating fast from the catwalk. "Did you get my text?"

"Yeah, I did," Alex said, sounding slightly annoyed. "But I got it too late. Xander and I were already waiting for you guys at Wollman."

"Oh, crap," I said. This was exactly what I did not want to happen. "Alex, I'm so sorry. I don't want to keep making excuses about my schedule this week, or else I might never stop. But will you two *please* come to this fashion show tomorrow night?"

"I don't know," Alex said. His voice sounded strained. "I guess I have to see how long lacrosse practice goes tomorrow afternoon. And I definitely can't make any promises for Xander."

I sighed. I was in trouble with way too many people who were important to me right now. "Well, I really hope you can make it."

Alex cleared his throat, and a long moment of

silence passed, during which I heard Jade yell out, "Where is Flan? I need her!"

"Sounds like you gotta get going," Alex finally said. "Maybe I'll see you tomorrow."

"Fingers crossed," I said quietly, suddenly feeling like the essence of a bad friend.

Chapter 23

*T*oo few hours of sleep and a blink of a school day later, I was heading back to the Armory show—but this time, it was the real deal. To say that I was a little shaky would be an understatement, but most of the girls from the field hockey team had agreed to meet up outside Thoney after school to cab caravan over to the show, and it was good to have them for company. After conveying to Camille how much I'd lit into Alex to bring Xander to the show tonight, she'd agreed to kiss and make up. As she herded people into one taxi van, I squeezed in next to Ramsey in another.

"You know, Flan," she said to me as the cab turned onto Park, "I've never been to one of these Virgils before. Formal wear's not really my thing. But with you running it tomorrow, I just might decide to check it out."

I looked over at Ramsey's baseball-capped head and felt glad for her vote of confidence. Given the way she brought our team together, her opinion meant a lot to me.

"Thanks, Ramsey," I said as the cab pulled to a stop in front of The Armory Show. "Now," I grinned at her, putting on my best Jade accent, "let's see what everyone will be wearing on ze field zis season."

At the door, I flashed my model badge then followed the team up the stairs. I knew the rest of our class would be trickling in later, but I wanted to make sure the field hockey girls got their special VIP seating in the front section.

"I'll just make sure you guys find your seats before I head to the dressing room," I said when we entered the hall.

Over the arch of the runway, giant shimmering white letters spelled out JADE. The walls and ceiling had been decorated to look like a cross between an underwater scene and the moon. There were American flags planted into what looked like lunar craters lining the runway. A gauzy blue drape of fabric dipped down from the ceiling. It seemed like an odd backdrop to showcase field hockey uniforms—even haute evening wear field hockey uniforms. Jade was either a genius or a total wacko. But when I looked at the mesmerized faces of my teammates, I decided she was probably a genius.

Just then, I felt a jerk on my left elbow, and I turned to see a panic-stricken Jade. Her face was white against her red lipstick.

"*Chérie*," she hissed. "I need your help. These models, they are *impossible*. I ask them for one simple change, and they revolt against me! You must reason with them."

Before I could respond, she'd yanked me backstage. In the dressing room, the models were packing up their bags.

"What is this?" Jade yelled. "You cannot strike on day of show."

The "morphology" model shrugged. "I will say in English so Blond Essence and everyone can understand. *You* think we cannot strike? Maybe *you* cannot order us to memorize words that are *complètement impossible* one day then change them at no warning. We quit."

"You quit?" I asked, still not believing my ears.

"*Oui*," Morphology nodded. "Learning how to say 'clairvoyance' in *une heure? Non!* We are finished here." She struggled with "clairvoyance" a few more times under her breath, but each time, it came bumbling out. "Klar . . . vwah . . . yunce." Finally, she glanced sideways at the bearded members of the jazz band playing poker in the corner. "You know what else, Jade Moodswing?" she said. "We're taking our boyfriends with us. Come on, Pierre. Jean. Luc. *Allons-y*."

Jade's mouth dropped open and she started fanning herself with the fashion show's program. She turned to me, stunned silent, as one by one, model and musician made their way out the back door in a single file line.

Jade fell against a wall and looked completely stricken. "*Aide-moi*," she finally managed to whisper to me. I looked around the empty dressing room.

"Okay," I said, trying to keep my voice even so Jade wouldn't know how in over my head I was feeling. "There has to be an easy solution to this. We just need to score some models and some music, right? Piece of cake."

"Um, Flan—" Camille's auburn head popped into the dressing room, and she did not look happy. "There's a bit of a problem outside. We need you . . . fast."

I turned to Jade and handed her a bottle of water from my bag. "Stay here. Drink this. Don't worry," I said. "I'll be right back with a solution."

I left Jade and followed Camille out to the drill hall, where a large military-looking security guard was lording over the section of chairs where our team was supposed to be sitting. His chubby face was red and angry, and he was shaking his finger emphatically at Ramsey. Even his flashlight looked scary.

"Are these *your* guests, ma'am?" he asked me gruffly, like I'd brought a bunch of wild dogs into a Michelin Guide–starred restaurant.

"Um, yes," I said, looking at everyone's school bags and hockey clothes strewn around the aisles. I was starting to realize why he was so worked up. "Is there a problem?" I asked innocently.

"Only that you're breaking about eight fire codes in here. For one thing, all these hockey sticks need to be taken out of here, stat. And you've got way too many people trying to squeeze into this section. Who's responsible for the guest list?"

I bit my lip. I didn't want to lay any more pressure on Jade, who'd handled all the seating, so I looked into the bright flashlight of the security guard, took a deep breath, and said, "I am. If you'll just give me five minutes, I'm sure I can figure out a way to—"

A snicker to my left interrupted me.

"Poor Flan," Kennedy said, shaking her head. She looked flawless in a black sequined cocktail dress and Louboutin slides. "Cardinal rule number one. Didn't anyone ever tell you there's a reason why some events are exclusive? Inviting the whole world to a fashion show just to win some stupid election . . . well, it's naïve, and frankly a little bit pathetic. Guess you're learning that the hard way."

"Unfortunately," an equally nasty voice said, "fashion show seating is the least of Flan's problems." I spun around to see Willa standing with her Razr at her ear. Her yellow Alice + Olivia shift dress shimmered under the Armory's show lighting, and her ears dripped with gorgeous aquamarine drop earrings. She snapped her phone shut in her palm and put her hand on my shoulder. "I just got off the phone with Headmistress Winters. She wanted me, as class president, to be the one to tell you." She paused dramatically, giving me enough time to wish we were on the field and I could hip check her.

"What are you talking about, Willa?" I said.

"What was the one thing you were supposed to do as Virgil Host?" she said, holding up a perfectly manicured index finger.

I racked my brain. I'd won the election, and then—

"Need a clue? You forgot to confirm with the caterer. We can't have a Virgil without food," Willa said, shaking her head. "I have to say, Headmistress was not pleased when the Boathouse called to say that the special events caterer canceled. Maybe you should have thought about your tendency to choke under pressure before you ran for Host and let everyone down." She folder her arms over her chest. "What's next, Flan? Are you the treasury thief, too?"

Around me, I heard the rest of our team gasp. Sure, I'd been a little forgetful this week, but accusing me of stealing from Thoney? That was a low blow.

I didn't even know what to say, but at that moment, I also didn't have a chance. Jade surprise attacked me, both of her skinny hands gripping my elbows.

"You've been gone for six minutes," she moaned. "What am I doing for models? What am I doing for music? Get me Feb!"

I sighed and took a full glimpse at the mayhem surrounding me: panicked designer to my left, bitchy nemesis duo to my right, field hockey team about to be thrown out by the scary security guard. And everyone was looking right back at me, waiting for answers.

My head started spinning—until my eyes fell on Camille's tote bag and Morgan's CD—the FLAN'S GOT YOU COVERED mix—sticking out of it.

And *voilà*—music! Slowly, everything started to fall into place in my mind. Now I just had to pull it off.

I pulled the CD out of Camille's bag and handed it to Jade.

"This is perfect for the show," I told her. "We don't need a band at all—we just need a stereo system.

"As for models . . ." I paused, scanning my teammates' faces. "Have you ever seen fourteen more beautiful, graceful—all-American—girls?" I asked Jade. "Who better to model the transformation of the uniforms than girls who'll actually be wearing them?"

Jade nodded like she was starting to see where I was coming from. Better yet, I could see the girls on the team bobbing with excitement about the chance to walk the runway in a fashion show.

"And if you guys want to walk," I said to the team as they edged closer to me, nodding, "you just have to promise to do me one tiny little favor after the show."

"Anything," Ramsey said.

"Help me cook up a storm tonight. If we want to have Virgil, we might have to take catering matters into our own hands."

Camille nodded, apparently coming around to the idea. "I do make a mean bruschetta."

As the other girls on the team chimed in with recipes they'd be happy to contribute, a look of relief washed over Jade's face.

"You're either cuckoo or a genius, *chérie*," she said.

I turned to the security guard. "And that'll take care of the fire hazard, because we'll move everything and everyone backstage, so you don't even have to call the fire marshal."

Now the only gloomy faces in the group were Kennedy's and Willa's, and for some reason, that didn't bother me at all.

"You guys want to be in the show or what?" I asked them, and I got silent stares at the ground. They didn't look like they were going anywhere. "That's what I thought," I said. "I'll let your ridiculous accusation about the school funds slide this time, Willa. And Virgil's still on, that's for sure."

"And it's going to rock, that's for *sure*." Camille backed me up.

"All the models—backstage," Jade's voice rang out from her headset microphone. She was back in power-pout mode. "We only have ten minutes to get you fitted and memorizing your words!"

Ramsey shot me a confused look. "Our words?" she said.

"Don't ask." I laughed as we picked up our sticks and started to book it to the dressing room. "Just be glad English is your first language."

Chapter 24

"Clairvoyance," I heard Ramsey belt out when she got to the head of the runway in her bejeweled floor-length field hockey uniform. She'd successfully kicked off Jade's show, and I could hear the *oohs* and *aahs* from the crowd to prove it.

I was backstage, huddled up with my designer teammates, all of us jittery with pre-walk excitement. My heart was beating fast, but as I looked around me, I had to remind myself that at least I'd had a dress rehearsal for this. The rest of my teammates were basically winging it. At least they looked incredible.

Sure, we'd gotten off to a slightly late start. The lights went down and came back up, and we were still running around backstage, hustling to get all fourteen girls outfitted and altered and lined up at the door. But it was better to walk late than never, and I had to admit, I'd never seen a better-looking field hockey team or a more dazzling group of models.

Ramsey looked spectacular, all aglow when she returned from her foray on the catwalk. I'd been a bit surprised that Jade had seized on her to be the opening model for the collection, but that, too, was part of her genius.

She'd said, "There's such strength in you. You are the perfect debut for my line. You will *be* the sportswear evening gown, *non*?"

Now the lights in the drill hall were out except for the headlights over the bright white runway and the flash of the photographers' cameras. Morgan's CD sounded great blaring through the Bose stereo system that Feb was controlling upstairs. I really hoped Morgan was in the audience now with Harper and Amory, and that she was jazzed to hear her music being used as the soundtrack for the show. I didn't want to be a one-hit wonder, and I knew that after my flakiness this week, playing Morgan's CD wasn't enough to get my friendship batting average back up to where it had started with those girls. Still, I had to hope it was at least a base hit.

As my teammates entered the runway one by one, I kept my fingers crossed that everyone's spin around the catwalk would go off without a hitch. Thank goodness the Thoney girls had been more receptive to spouting off multisyllabic words at the head of the runway than their French counterparts had been.

"Elemental," I heard Jenna, our blond forward, enunciate perfectly when she reached the end of the catwalk.

Camille was up next. I sneaked out of line for a minute to squeeze her hand. "Good luck, Ms. Onomatopoeia," I whispered.

She grinned at me. "You too, Ms. Essence."

From where I stood backstage, I could barely see Camille's willowy frame as she entered the hall, but through the gauzy backdrop, I could hear that a section in the audience had given her an enthusiastic standing ovation when she unleashed "Onomatopoeia" on them. I kept my fingers crossed that Xander was out there somewhere with Alex.

Before I knew it, almost all the girls had filed on and off the runway. In front of me was just Willa and Kennedy. Turns out they'd both decided their shot at modeling was more important than consistency in their bitchiness.

All three of us shared a nervous glance, which felt a little funny, because sure, ninety percent of the time the vibe between us bordered on destructive. But tonight, none of that was on my mind. I only wanted the show to go off without a hitch. I genuinely hoped both of them had great walks—for their sake, for Jade's sake, and for the sake of our whole field hockey team.

"Good luck out there, you guys," I said.

Neither one of them said anything, but both of them nodded at me in an *almost* agreeable way.

"Kennedy," Jade's PA hissed, "you're up."

The music changed to a slower Meiko song, the last song of the show. I'd been listening to it a lot on my iPod since Morgan had given me this CD, to the point that its catchy electronic beat was already tied in my mind to the insanity of my first week at Thoney.

"Determination," Kennedy called out, posing at the end of runway and getting a peppy round of applause.

Willa turned back and gave me a quick smile before she strutted out through the curtains. As they billowed back behind her, I got a glimpse of what it looked like outside. The entire place was packed.

"Solidarity," Willa announced to the crowd.

In the jumbled assignments of words, I hadn't been sure what word had been given to whom, but "solidarity" seemed both ironic and fitting for Willa. I didn't know if this moment of semi-truce among the three of us would last, or whether we were all just caught up in the exhilaration of the moment, but I didn't have time to dwell on it. I was up. And suddenly, I was terrified.

There was no snooty French model to nudge me onto the runway, but I felt the cue in the music and began to walk. My first step was a little wobbly, but when I got into full view of everyone on the runway, I was overwhelmed by how incredible I felt. And then I just let go. In a blinding flash of lights, I somehow made it to the end of the runway.

"Essence," I said calmly, evenly, in a voice that didn't match how jittery I'd been feeling seconds earlier. The flashes from the photographers popped even brighter in my eyes, and I did my best not to break into a crazy grin. And when a large section of the crowd burst into a cheer, I looked over and could make out the faces of my family, all sprung from their seats and clapping. I was so excited to see them that— I couldn't help myself—I gave a little wave. It may not have been the most professional model behavior, but let's face it, as fun as this had been, I made a better field hockey player—and a better sister and daughter and friend—than I did a model any day. I didn't have to be able to see my mother's face clearly to know that she was crying.

Backstage again, all my friends were caught up in a

wave of frantic hugs and kisses. There were choruses of "You walked so well!" and "No, *you* did!"

Jade was beaming.

"You did a fantastic job, *chérie*," I said, giving her the double cheek kiss.

"I couldn't have done it without your essence," she said, air-kissing each of my cheeks twice—the ultimate display of French approval. "Shall we enter the throngs of the public eye to be showered by praises? That is always my favorite part."

The main hall was crawling with journalists, photographers, and news crews. I posed for a few pictures with Jade and with my teammates, but mostly, I was looking for my family and my friends.

Luckily, I didn't have to wait too long to find the Floods. All at once, four massive bouquets of roses came at me and, above them, I found the beaming faces of my parents and my siblings.

"You were wonderful, darling," my mom said with a huge smile. "We have to run to make dinner reservations, but we'll see you at home later."

Feb even took off her headset to say, "Jade told me how clutch you were, Flan. I must say, I taught you well."

"Thanks, Feb, I learned from the best." I grinned and turned to Patch. "Aren't you supposed to be in the Czech Republic?"

"Not till tomorrow," he said, giving me a hug. "Rumor has it you've been rocking the student body at Thoney."

"Where'd you hear that?" I asked.

Patch stepped aside and put his arm around Shira Riley, who looked a whole lot less intimidating now that she was smiling at me with my brother's arm around her waist.

On the other side of Shira was Anna Altfest, who leaned in for a cheek kiss and said, "Congrats, babe. It's about time someone took a stance on those hideous hockey uniforms. You guys are going to look so great out there. Spence won't have a chance."

"Thanks, Anna," I said. "Thanks, everyone."

Seeing Anna made me realize that, as psyched as I was to have my family's support, there was still one other person I was holding out for tonight.

"Hey, Anna," a guy's voice from behind her said. "I barely get enough time with this girl as it is. Think you could quit hogging Flan for just a second?"

"Alex," I said, not even trying to rein in my huge smile. "You made it."

"Yeah, well." He looked down at the ground. "I was never *really* going to miss it. Just kinda had to keep you guessing," he said. "You know, Guy Rule Number One."

"I thought you didn't believe in rules," I teased.

"Some things are worth following the rules for," he said, giving me a hug. "That is, if you really want them. Now check out what's developing over there." He pointed behind me to the short staircase leading up to the stage where Xander was chatting up Camille. He must have been saying something hilarious, because she was totally cracking up.

"Could either one of them be more beet red?" Alex asked me, laughing.

"Definitely not," I said. Just then, the lights in the drill hall slowly came up to coax everyone outside. "Thanks for bringing Xander along," I said as Alex helped me into my coat.

"Sure," Alex said. "I'd like to say it was hard work and that you owe me big time, but really, it wasn't that tough to convince him. All I had to do was mention Camille's name."

The crowd was gathering outside on the freezing January street.

"So what are you up to now?" Alex asked. "No more big plans for tonight, I hope?"

"Actually," I said, "it turns out I have to put in one more crazy night preparing for Virgil tomorrow, but after that . . ." I trailed off.

"After that . . ." Alex paused. He smiled at me. "Are

you saying that after you do whatever secret Virgil planning you have to do tonight, and after the big event tomorrow . . . are you actually suggesting, Flan Flood, that I might get to hang out with you?"

I laughed. "That might be what I'm saying."

"Well, then," Alex said, tossing his scarf around his neck and putting up his hand to hail me a taxi, "I guess I'll just have to wait one more night."

When the cab dropped me off on my stoop, I raced inside to see what kind of shape our kitchen was in for an all-night cooking affair. Luckily, the Flood household was spotless and—not surprisingly—empty.

I cranked up Morgan's CD, turned on some mood lighting, and made my slumber party specialty— popcorn mixed with M&M's and almonds. Ramsey and the girls were stopping by Zabar's to pick up supplies, so I figured if I were bringing a crew of midnight helpers over, I should at least give them the royal treatment.

When the doorbell rang, I stepped outside to let in Camille, Ramsey, and the rest of the field hockey team. Everyone had brought pajamas, and each girl carried a bag of groceries.

"Chef service!" Camille called out. "Sort of like room service, except you have to do all the work."

"Thank you guys so much for coming over," I said, showing everyone inside. I was just about to shut the door when I saw three more figures approaching my stoop. As they climbed up the stairs, I realized it was Harper, Amory, and Morgan, each carrying a bag of groceries.

"We heard you were catering Virgil yourself," Harper said, shaking her head. "Have you ever heard of taking it easy?"

"Seriously," Amory agreed.

"I don't cook," Morgan admitted. "But I will late-night DJ to keep the troops energized for the long haul."

"The more the merrier." I laughed. "And we can definitely use a DJ."

"Okay, team," I heard Ramsey call out from the kitchen. When I led Harper, Amory, and Morgan inside, she was sitting on the counter with a clipboard in her lap. "Let's huddle up and talk strategy." Apparently, Ramsey was as unstoppable in the kitchen as she was on the hockey field. "We'll have four stations: appetizers, salads, mains, and desserts. We'll divvy up the ingredients, make menus, coordinate oven times, and make this thing happen. Are you with me?"

And so, at ten thirty on Thursday night, twenty

exhausted girls huddled up, and not even Camille groaned about the strategizing.

Within minutes, my kitchen, which had never in its life seen so much action, was transformed into a serious work zone. A cloud of flour rose up over the dessert section as the girls set to work cutting out pastry shells for fruit tarts. Ramsey stood on her tiptoes and oversaw the glazing of the teriyaki tofu. Camille demonstrated the best way to seed the tomatoes for her famous bruschetta. Harper pulled out some amazing skills toasting nuts for the salads she'd decided we would serve in coffee cups. Morgan donned a large pair of Patch's DJ headphones and pumped us up by mixing some energetic techno beats. And I took breaks from my role assisting Camille on the garlic chopping and walked around the kitchen holding out the bowl of magic popcorn to anyone who needed an extra boost.

By midnight, the kitchen was a disaster, but we were halfway through the preparation. Camille came up and put her arm around me. "When Willa dropped that bomb on you tonight, I never thought I'd get to say this . . . but I think we just might pull this crazy idea off."

Just then, the doorbell rang, and Camille and I shared a confused look.

"You don't think that's Willa and Kennedy, do you?" I asked. They were the only two members of the hockey team not representing at my house tonight. "I thought we sort of had a moment on the runway tonight. Maybe they're—"

Camille raised an eyebrow at me. "What," she said, "maybe they've stopped being agents of evil? I don't know, Flan, I wouldn't get your hopes up. People are different on and off the runway."

I went to the door with no idea what I'd be confronted with, and what I found was even more startling than a contrite Kennedy and Willa.

"SBB!" I cried. "Oh my God, what happened to you?"

She looked like she'd been through Hell and back again. Her blond hair was matted to her face, and her cream colored dress was lopsided and falling off her shoulder—and suddenly, I realized it was all my fault.

"Oh no!" I said, covering my face with my flour-covered hands.

"You forgot about me. I left you twenty-seven messages, but you still forgot about me," she peeped before collapsing at my feet. "And now my life is over."

"Oh, SBB," I said. "I'm *so* sorry. The show ran late, and my phone was off . . ." I held out my arms and helped her inside the living room, away from the chaos of the kitchen. "What happened?"

"What *didn't* happen?" she wailed. "I couldn't get a hold of you. I stopped by and no one was here except for Patch, who told me not to go with the Nanette Lepore. I realize now I should *never* listen to Patch's opinion on fashion, but I couldn't help it! He was the closest thing I could find to you. And so I ditched the first dress we'd agreed on, and I went with this ridiculous Gucci ensemble." She flicked the gorgeous satin gown at her hips. "Huge mistake," she said, looking up at me with big, mascara-streaked eyes.

"Ashleigh Ann?" I asked, feeling my heart drop into my stomach. Sure, SBB had a tendency to over-dramatize the situation, but this one sounded real, and I was scared to hear whether her biggest fears had actually come true.

SBB nodded. "Same Jimmy Choo shoes, same Gucci dress, same Versace clutch. Grade A red carpet disaster. *And* she showed up first, effectively ruining my reputation. I was the copycat. There was nothing to be done."

"Oh SBB—"

"*And then,*" she said, not letting me finish, "Gloria showed up and forced me to have dinner with her at Per Se. JR got sucked into a brainstorming meeting with Garrison Toyota, and I was left alone—*alone*—with the woman who continues to lord over me the fact the she gave me life. She spent at least an hour trying to bribe me into letting her have custody of me again. The nerve, Flan, the absolute *nerve*! It could not have been more of a disaster." She turned to look at me with her big blue eyes, and I felt like just as much of an irresponsible mother as Gloria. "Why weren't you there, Flan?" SBB pleaded. "My career is basically over, so I've got all the time in the world to listen to your excuse."

Just then, Ramsey poked her head into the living room. "Flan, can you taste this sauce?" she asked. "Wait, aren't you Sara-Beth Benny?"

SBB sighed. "I used to be," she said, shooting me a look. "Now I am a shadow of my former self, no thanks to Flan. I'll taste the sauce."

Ramsey shrugged and put the wooden spoon to SBB's lips.

SBB savored the sauce for a minute, then said, "Hmm. Add a touch of salt, some rosemary, maybe cut it with a little honey. Overall, I think it's pretty good. But"—she wagged a menacing finger at me—"*we* are not good."

As I watched her huddled figure plod to my front door before slamming it behind her, my heart twisted up. I couldn't believe I'd let my best friend down. As I plopped down on the couch, I thought: I had to figure out a way to make it up to her.

"Flan," Camille called out from the kitchen, "we need you. We can't figure out how to work the blow torch for the chocolate crème brûlée."

"I'll be right there." I sighed and heaved myself off the couch. Tomorrow, I thought. I'll have to figure it all out tomorrow.

Chapter 26

$\mathcal{B}$y the time the clock struck two a.m., twenty-four trays had been filled with yummy Virgil-worthy noshes, and Ramsey, Harper, Amory, and Morgan were drying the last of the non-dishwasher-safe dishes.

"You guys are lifesavers," I said as the four of them lined up at the door to put on their coats and scarves.

"No sweat," Amory said. "It's good practice for when I audition for the role of Cinderella. See you tomorrow!"

Back in the kitchen, Camille was pulling one final tray of brownies out of the oven.

"Last women standing," I said.

Camille laid the brownies on a trivet, tossed both oven mitts over her shoulder, and started cracking up.

"What's so funny?" I said.

"I have no idea," she wheezed, gripping her sides.

215

"Nothing. I'm just slap happy from the amount of food produced in this kitchen in one night."

"I don't think it will ever happen again," I said, shaking my head. "I can't wait to tell my mom that someone finally figured out how to use the oven without singeing anything in the process."

"Do we have any more of that magic popcorn left?" Camille asked, looking around the kitchen.

"I'll make another batch," I said, picking up the empty bowl.

"Don't bother," Camille said. "I'm just used to snacking on that when we gossip. But I don't know if I can even look at any more food. It's probably better if we both just collapse."

"Wait," I said, "does that mean we finally get to gossip, even if there's no magic popcorn to get us going?"

"Well"—Camille sighed dramatically—"I guess we probably should."

We crawled to the living room and each claimed one of the brown suede couches. I tossed Camille a blanket and we put on old TiVoed episodes of *Gossip Girl* to set the mood.

"So, did you see him kiss me?" Camille asked, squirming into her pillow.

"He *kissed* you?" I squealed.

"*Shhh*! What if someone hears?" Camille said, looking around the empty living room.

As soon as she realized how completely irrational that fear was, we both busted out laughing. We laughed so hard that we started crying, which always happened to us at the exact same time. Just as we were finally calming down, a panicked thought popped into my head.

"Camille," I said, shooting up on the couch.

"What is it?" she asked. "Don't tell me you made some other plans tonight that you forgot about?"

"No," I said. "This time, I'm actually planning ahead. How in the world are we going to get all this food to Virgil?"

At that instant, my front door burst open, and Patch sauntered in wearing a top hat and a tuxedo. Next to him stood a guy in a large puffy black coat with a pulled up fur-trimmed hood and dark sunglasses.

"What are you doing up, Flan?" Patch said. "Figured you'd be conked out after your big runway event." He motioned to his mysterious companion. "You know Jake Riverdale, right?"

I squinted at the masked man. When he removed his hood and his shades to reveal his gorgeous pop star face and trademark dimpled smile, I had to do a double take. I mean, I'd spent months of my life talking *about* JR with SBB, but until this moment I'd never actually met him.

"What's up, little Flood," he said, shaking his head. "Wait, are you the famous Flan my girl is always raving about?"

"Um, I used to be," I said, feeling another wave of guilt wash over me. "But probably not anymore. SBB was pretty upset with me tonight," I rambled, suddenly aware that I was in the incredibly hot presence of *the* JR. Camille was practically hyperventilating next to me. "And I deserved it—"

"Don't sweat it," JR said. "I think she was just frantic about seeing Gloria. I'm already in hot water with her for ducking out on dinner. If anyone has groveling to do, it's me. I think I'm going to go over to her house tomorrow morning, make her breakfast, and see if she'll agree to let me take her out tomorrow night—"

"Wait a minute," I said, holding up a finger. "I think I have an idea."

"Does your idea include JR and me chowing down on some of whatever smells so good in the kitchen?" Patch said. "I'm starving."

"No," I said sternly. "We did not cook all night for you to tear through our hors d'oeuvres in five minutes. We need that stuff for tomorrow—if we can figure out a way to get it there."

"I'll make you a deal," Patch said. "You let JR and me have a very small sample of your fancy food, and I'll call a friend who can arrange to get everything delivered to your party."

"Okay," I said. "But only one bite each!"

"Dude," JR said as he and Patch headed into the kitchen. "She always this bossy? Is that where SBB learns it?"

But whatever Patch had to say about my bossiness fell on deaf ears, because just then my head hit the pillow, and I fell fast asleep.

The afternoon sun was glinting off the Central Park pond when Camille and I arrived at the Boathouse. Patch was already there, directing a crew of three burly guys to start unloading the truck.

"Let's get the hot stuff in there first," he called out as they hoisted our trays on their shoulders with surprising professionalism—given that they were Patch's friends—and started filing into the Boathouse Café.

"Um, speaking of hot stuff," Camille said, giving me a look.

"Yeah, Patch, where'd you find these guys?" I asked.

"I know, right?" Patch said, smiling impishly. "They handle all the heavy lifting for events at the Rainbow Room. I met them in Rio and they let me crash during Carnival. I'm telling you, caterer dudes know how to party."

It was almost too easy to watch them work, and a half hour later, the food was all strategically placed around the room. Soon, the winter white flower arrangements were brought in, and the DJ was setting up in the corner.

One of the Brazilian guys came up and put his arms around Camille and me. "You American girls really know how to throw down with style," he said, grabbing a bottle of water from the bar.

"Thanks," I said, smiling and thinking of my single friends. "You guys should totally stick around for Virgil."

By five o'clock, Camille and I were in the bathroom changing into our dresses. I zipped up the back of her floor-length red silk Bill Blass gown and helped her arrange the cap sleeves so they lay just right against her naturally tanned shoulders.

"Gorgeous. Have you ever considered a career in modeling?" I joked.

"Tried it once," Camille laughed. "But I think we have more fun *off* the catwalk."

"You know, I'm never taking this dress off," I said, running my hands down the amazing Zac Posen dress SBB had given me. It was the perfect cut: a princess neckline and a full skirt that made me feel as light as air.

Unfortunately, I couldn't help feeling weighed down when I thought about SBB's crestfallen face last night. I crossed my fingers that the plan I'd texted JR about this morning would get things with us back to normal.

"Hey," Camille said, grabbing my arm. "Look who's here!"

As we watched the buses from Dalton and Thoney arrive and unload chatty groups of guys and girls, we scooted toward the coat check to be the first to greet everyone.

The first person I spotted was Mattie Hendricks, looking sweet in a simple A-line black dress.

"Hey, Mattie," I said, leaning in for a kiss.

"Flan, oh my God, how did you pull this off? It's so beautiful!"

"Thanks, Mattie," I said, handing her one of the specialty virgin cocktails Camille and I had come up with, with a little help from the Brazilian boys. "Have a Thoney Torpedo. It's açaí, pineapple, and coconut. Cheers!"

As the room started to fill up with happy, top-of-the-weekend chatter, I hung around the entryway, passing out Torpedos and compliments on everyone's amazing gowns.

"Faiden," I said, admiring her pale pink bubble

dress. "Who are you wearing? It's gorgeous," I said, sort of feeling like an interviewer on E!

"Actually," she said, taking a little spin so I could see the back, "I made it. I got a sewing machine for Christmas, and this was my first project."

"Wow," I said. "I'm so impressed."

"So am I," I heard a poised voice say behind me. I turned around to find Headmistress Winters standing next to Mr. Zimmer. "Flan," she said, "you've done an excellent job. In just one week, you have shown us all just what it is that makes the Thoney spirit such a wonderful thing. Your extracurricular endeavors are commendable, and what's more"—she smiled at Mr. Zimmer—"Mr. Zimmer tells me you've got a true zeal for academics. I was pleased to hear that you've taken such an interest in your English studies."

"Thank you," I said, blushing. "It's been a great two weeks."

"We're certainly lucky to have you join us this semester," Mr. Zimmer agreed. "Now, if you'll excuse us," he said, steering the headmistress toward the bar. "I believe it's time for us to try this famous Torpedo everyone is raving about."

"Whoa," Camille said, coming up behind me. "*Zimmer and Winters*? They're totally smitten with each other. I had no idea." We both started cracking up. "It's kind of adorable, don't you think?"

"Spoken like a girl who's so smitten herself that she thinks *everyone* in love is cute," I teased. "I'm onto you."

"Point taken. Love is cute." She laughed. "*Especially* these two walking in right now." Camille pointed toward the door. I followed her finger and saw the familiar flash of a green Nanette Lepore dress arm-in-arm with a black Marc Jacobs tuxedo.

"SBB," I called, checking her face for signs of residual anger. "You made it!"

But SBB threw her arms around me. "Congrats on such a sweet party, Flan. This is just the sort of thing that makes me wish I'd gone to high school."

"I'm so glad you're here," I said. "And I'm so sorry again about—"

SBB put up her hand. "Please. That was, what, twenty hours ago? Over and done with. When JR surprised me with breakfast in bed this morning, I figured you might have had a hand in it. And—" She leaned forward to show me the new platinum locket she was wearing. It was almost identical to the Shakespearean one she'd given me last week, but it had a gorgeous yellow diamond at its center. She popped it open, and inside, it read, *The fairest starlet in all of heaven.*

Phew. So JR *had* followed my instructions.

"I *know* you had a hand in this," SBB continued, waving her metallic clutch in the air. "And I love, love, love, *love* it. And I love you, Flannie." She turned to JR. "And I love you, too, schnookums."

JR leaned in to kiss SBB, looking the definition of smitten.

Just then I felt a tap on my shoulder. I turned around, hoping to see Alex. All these other couples were making me a little bit anxious to hip check him. . . .

"Sorry to interrupt, Flan," said the opposite of Alex. "I need to talk to you."

It was Willa, and judging from the look on her face, she seemed to have erased from her brain whatever bonding moment we might have had last night. She was flanked by Kennedy and Headmistress Winters, who looked decidedly less thrilled with me than she had five minutes ago. Suddenly the only thing in the air was a black cloud hanging over the entryway.

"What's going on?" I asked.

"We knew you weren't familiar enough with Thoney protocol to host," Willa sneered.

"We should have known when you forgot to call the caterer," Kennedy said, shaking her head. "The little . . . snacks you produced are a really nice effort, but homemade sandwiches are not exactly appropriate for a formal event."

"But the real offense," Willa picked up, "is your flimsy open door policy. Rumor has it there are strange foreign men running rampant through the crowd and making everyone very uncomfortable. And apparently you weren't even going to stop there." She pointed in SBB and JR's direction. "Are you just going to let *everyone* in off the street?"

It was such a ridiculous thing to say about two of the world's most celebrated actors that I was absolutely stunned silent.

Luckily, SBB was not. She tilted her head, pointed at Willa's outfit, and said, "That's a very familiar Gucci dress. It costs, what, about three thousand dollars? I should know—I wore the same one last night." She turned to me, and I wondered where she was going with this. "Flan, didn't you say that was the exact amount missing from the class treasury? And is this the same Willa you said was serving her school as class president?" Then SBB put on her perfected Shakespearean pout. "Methinks the school may be serving Willa more than she's serving the school."

Mr. Zimmer tilted his head. "Well spoken, young lady," he said.

Willa opened her mouth and closed it three times before she clutched her fists together and lunged at SBB. Just before she pounced on my best friend, JR caught her by the wrists.

"Nobody messes with my girlfriend," he said. I could have sworn he had the same line in *Derelict Dudes,* but it had the same swoon-worthy effect in the movie as it did with his off-screen costar.

"You don't know who you're messing with," Willa hissed, flailing her arms in vain against JR's grasp. "You just wait until my father finds out about this. My family blows our nose with three thousand dollars. I swear"—she glared at me—"you've got the wrong girl."

"That's not what our night cameras found out, Willa," Headmistress Winters announced, steering her out by her shoulders. "We were hoping you'd come forward of your own volition, but now you're just making a scene. You've got a problem with honesty, Willa, and we've known about it for some time. You can give us your full deposition in the privacy of my office."

We stood around and watched as Willa was literally dragged out of the Boathouse. Kennedy trailed behind her like a dog with her tail between her legs. When both of them were gone, the room fell silent, and the rest of us let out giant sighs.

"The excitement never ends at Thoney," Camille said, rolling her eyes. "Aren't you glad you decided to come back, Flan?"

"Willa's witchiness aside," I said, linking my arm through hers and SBB's, "I really am. But Camille, can you do me one favor?"

"Anything for the hostess with the mostest," she said.

"*Never* let me run for one of these things again. This party's been fun, but so is ice skating in the park, and that's a whole lot less work."

"Deal," Camille said with a nod. "Hey, look who it is!"

The Boathouse doors swung open and my Prince of New York walked in with Xander at his side. Both of them looked very dapper in their matching charcoal tuxes.

"Hey, you," Alex said, melting me with his smile. "What'd we miss? I'm sorry we're so late."

"Actually," I said, "you're right on time. I think we should all get out of here. Who wants to go to the park and go skating?"

"Flan, I love you," SBB said, getting moderately huffy again. "But I did *not* put on this dress just to take it off again."

"SBB's right," Camille said. "Which is why I suggest . . . the first annual post-Virgil formal wear ice-skating event."

"Ooh," Xander said, leaning in to give Camille a big kiss right in front of us. "I like the way this girl thinks."

I grinned at Alex. "Are you up for it?" I asked.

Alex put his arms around me. A smile spread across his face. "It sounds like the start of a brand-new tradition." He gave me a slow kiss on the lips. "Come on, let's get you a cocktail."

I looked around the glittering Boathouse at all of my glittering friends, and thought, "There's absolutely nowhere in the world I'd rather be."

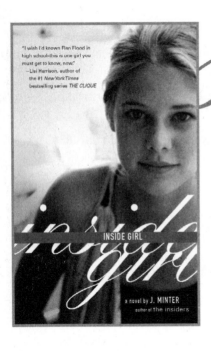

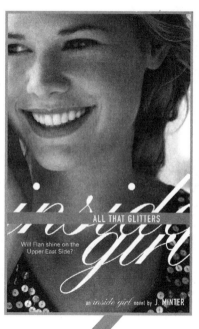

Can these guys' lives get *any* crazier? Get the whole scoop with the Insiders series!

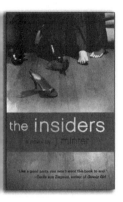

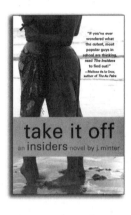

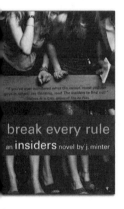

"The Insiders are *the* guys to watch. But if you fall in love with them, get in line, right behind ME!" —Zoey Dean, author of *The A-List*